THE LONELY BELOW

SCHOLASTIC PRESS I NEW YORK

All rights reserved. Published by Scholastic Press, an imprint of Scholastic Inc., *Publishers since 1920.* SCHOLASTIC, SCHOLASTIC PRESS, and associated logos are trademarks and/or registered trademarks of Scholastic Inc.

Library of Congress Cataloging-in-Publication Data available

ISBN 978-1-338-82512-1

10 9 8 7 6 5 4 3 2 1   24 25 26 27 28

Printed in the USA   61
First edition, August 2024

Book design by Omou Barry

FOR NORAH AND SHIRLEY

CHAPTER 0

As soon as the bathroom door clanged shut, my stomach dropped down into my toes. I could hear Theo's friends giggling on the other side. Being shoved into the haunted bathroom *alone* definitely didn't seem very funny to me. And when the dingy lights flickered and shut off, I felt like laughing even less.

The door didn't budge as I tried to pull it open, and panic was taking over. I was trapped.

In the dark.

Alone.

My palms ached from pounding against the door.

"Let me out!" I shouted. I didn't care that I sounded like a baby. I just wanted out.

Especially because I could feel a chill in the air that settled on my skin like silk.

The cold creeping in made me more frantic. I could feel something behind me, stalking toward me. The closer it got, the colder I felt.

"Theo!" I screamed. "There's something—"

Before I could finish, the cold surrounded me, choked me, pulled me down deep into it.

CHAPTER 1

TWO DAYS EARLIER

Grown folks had a real bad habit of talking *about* me instead of *to* me. Miss Pixie had already done it six times in the five minutes we'd been on this campus tour so far. I found myself invisible a lot, especially because sometimes I just couldn't talk around strangers. But Miss Pixie, with her giant perfect teeth and bouncy cheerleader ponytail, forgot I was around just as soon as she recognized my dad as an old classmate of hers from way back when they attended my new school together. I lagged behind them, even though the tour was supposed to be for me.

If I didn't like having to come to Blythe Academy before, I completely hated it now.

"You're very lucky, Les; a lot of parents would kill to get their kid into Blythe." Miss Pixie punctuated that statement with a shrill laugh and a quick touch to Daddy's arm.

She didn't notice, but I did—he leaned away just slightly with a little fake chuckle of his own. He was uncomfortable. I thought about how Dr. Choudhury would have been proud of me for putting that together. But then that made me think about how I wouldn't get to see my therapist in person for a while and how sad that made me. I slowed down even more, scuffing my sneakers on the gravel walkway.

Blythe Academy's campus sprawled beyond what I could see. The perfectly green grass and redbrick buildings reminded me of a college, even though they started accepting students as young as prekindergarten.

Most kids felt scared or nervous or sad starting a new school. I'd done it so often that it normally didn't bug me at all. But here, I felt claustrophobic. Like the giant magnolia trees all around had uprooted and crept slowly, slowly over to surround me. Their massive white blossoms stretched toward me like hands. My breath quickened. I lost sight of Daddy and Miss Pixie before I knew it. And the trees kept slinking closer.

A panic attack. I had learned years ago how to recognize when they were starting, and how to shorten them, but that didn't make them any less scary. I couldn't call out to Daddy—my throat refused to open up enough for words to come out. Waves of fear threatened to overtake me, to drown me, to make me feel like I was dying. Dr. Choudhury would have told me to keep breathing, find a way to ground myself, come back into the moment. So I stopped walking and sat down in the middle of the path and tried to press my palms firmly against the gravel to feel something solid.

Some students grumbled, annoyed, but their frustration didn't bother me the way it usually would during a meltdown. Instead of feeling embarrassed or weird, I just felt lost. Why hadn't Daddy turned and noticed I wasn't walking with them? Why was this stupid campus so big? And why were there so many dang trees?

I hadn't even moved into my new dorm yet and already my future at Blythe felt doomed. Normal kids at normal schools didn't have panic attacks or meltdowns. They didn't plop down in walkways and get dirty looks and refuse to speak or move or look at anyone. I *needed* to be normal. I needed to calm down.

But feeling so scared and nervous and stressed quickly turned into me forgetting if I'd ever felt calm before in my life. It felt impossible to remember what had helped calm me before. Music maybe? But none of my favorite songs came to mind. I couldn't distract myself with thoughts of adorable baby animals or a trip to an art supply store or memories of my sister letting me hang out with her in her room. I raised a hand to start rubbing my thumb against the cool metal of my necklace's locket.

MawMaw Septine had gifted it to me when I turned ten—a

thin-chained golden locket with a shiny oval opal embedded in the front of it. I felt proud that she trusted me with it. Inside was one coily ringlet from a Victorian-era ancestor. I'd forgotten over the years just how many greats into the past she was, and I felt too embarrassed to ask anyone. MawMaw Septine had gotten it from her grandmother, so at least two. She'd told me that there was nothing like feeling a connection to family to make you feel loved, or to keep you safe. Someday I hoped to pass it down to my own granddaughter. If I survived this panic attack. Which, at the moment, didn't seem possible.

My throat felt tight, the way it always did when I thought about MawMaw Septine. Nothing had been the same since she died two months ago. Nothing.

I didn't have a reason to cry, but my eyes didn't get that memo. Tears stung almost as much as the sharpness in my chest. This was it. I'd only just gotten to this new school, and I was going to drop dead of a heart attack right in the middle of the path.

As I tried to stop shaking and text Daddy that I needed him, a coldness wrapped around me. This didn't fit with any of my usual panic symptoms. With the cold came sadness, worry, and some unnameable feeling that made me tremble harder. No wind blew, and the sun shone and warmed the Mississippi air to an almost uncomfortably warm degree, but I wished I had my denim jacket to help with this chill.

A quick look around told me no one else was cold—no one was huddling deeper into their shirts or walking close together for warmth. All around, clusters of kids were laughing with each other, digging around in their backpacks, looking down at their phones. All the other students looked completely normal. No one looked like anything was wrong at all until my gaze landed on an extremely out of place woman staring at me from across the quad. She was nestled into a cluster of magnolia trees.

She stood tall. *Too* tall. Her face screwed up like she'd just smelled a really rank piece of rotten meat but was trying not to show it. Her blouse and long skirt looked like something a grandmother in a movie would wear. She had her hands tightly clasped in front of her, and her hair lay flat against her head and hung limply down her back and around her shoulders. She looked gaunt—a sad gray sheen to her glistening skin, caved-in cheeks, and a shine to her eyes.

More fitting than *gaunt*, my new favorite word: *ghastly*. My sister, Egypt, had bought me *The Gashlycrumb Tinies*, plus a bunch of other weird books, before she left for college. A bribe, Mama called it, so I wouldn't be upset over being left behind. I read it and reread it dozens of times to try and soothe myself whenever I missed her. We had talked about how when she was my age, she thought it said *ghastly* and explained to me what it meant. We spent the whole week before she left calling all

sorts of things ghastly—our cat Walter's poops, a tacky paint-
ing Mama found at a yard sale, some shoes at a store in the mall.
But this woman, this ghastly woman, fit the word best of all.
She looked just like one of Edward Gorey's creepy drawings.

The other kids ignored her—no talking, no waves, no
acknowledgment at all. Almost like they were afraid of her. But
I couldn't stop staring. Something about her . . .

As I stared, I forgot all about panicking, or losing the adults,
or even being cold. I tried to drag my eyes away from her but
couldn't. And as much as it scared me, neither did hers. But that
chill came back quickly as I watched her mouth start to move. I
shouldn't have been able to hear her from as far off as she was,
but her whispered voice slithered into my ear just as she began
to raise an arm. She aimed her index finger straight at me.

"*Home . . .*"

CHAPTER 2

I screamed and ducked my head as though if I couldn't see her, she couldn't see me. A hand touched my shoulder and I half expected to look up and see the ghastly woman. Instead, I saw my father. His deep, dark eyes stared into my own, almost like looking in a mirror. Except he's lighter than I am—high yella, Mama would say to tease him and Egypt—and I don't have a beard. He drew his hand back from me and placed it on his knee as he stooped beside me.

"Doodles, what happened?" he asked.

I didn't have an answer. All I had was nervousness in my stomach and the sinking feeling that I'd see the ghastly woman again if I looked anywhere other than at Daddy. When I didn't say anything, he reached to tuck one of my box braids back behind my ear.

"We can finish the tour later, if that would be easier," Miss Pixie said. Her voice softened the way grown folks' voices always did if they saw me melting down. I *hated* that voice.

The last time I heard it, my former teacher spoke to Mama about me, not *to* me, because I'd gotten overwhelmed on a field trip. Mama said she didn't need folks treating me with kid gloves or talking about me like I was a problem.

But that night, I heard Mama and Daddy talking. I heard them bicker over if it might be better to send me to a specialized school with teachers trained for interactions with disabled students. Before that, I hadn't heard either of them speak about me like I was different. And I swore that from then on I'd *never* give them a reason to fight about what to do with me again.

And yet here I sat, unable to speak, shaking and sweating, tears wetting up my shirt because I thought I saw something creepy among the trees. Disappointment started to crowd out panic in me.

"I think maybe we'll call it a day," Daddy said as he stood. "I can show her around later, after she gets settled in her room. This place hasn't changed too much from when I was a student here."

He lifted me up to carry me on his back and I felt like such a baby. I just knew other students were watching and laughing. Burying my head against Daddy's shoulder didn't make me feel as comforted as it normally would. I loved piggyback rides with my small number of trusted people, but here in front of other kids . . . I wanted to disappear.

"Okay," Miss Pixie said. Her smile felt full of pity, and she gently patted my back. "Well, Miss Eva, I look forward to having you in my dorm," she said. "I hope you get to feeling better."

I nodded. I hadn't wanted to live on campus at all to begin with, and now something about this place made my skin tingle, and not in the way it did when I listened to good music. Part of me felt angry at MawMaw Septine for dying, for this chain of events that kicked off after, for Mama and Daddy having to go take care of her things, leaving me behind. For the way her death made Mama, who was normally the loudest laugh at any gathering, disappear into grief so that any little inconvenience could turn her into a puddle of tears. But then I felt guilty for that even coming to my head at all.

"Thank you," Daddy said. He spoke for me pretty often and I always appreciated it, even if it made me feel like an even bigger baby. "Good seeing you, Pixie. We'll catch up."

He walked quietly to the car, adjusting me in his arms now and then. Once we reached the parking lot, he put me down and took hold of my hand.

"You wanna talk about what happened?" he asked. No judgment, or pity, or annoyance. Just a question. I loved that about him. Mama sometimes seemed frazzled when she talked to me after a meltdown, even though she wouldn't ever say so.

I climbed into the passenger seat, and the snap of my seat belt was the only sound I made. My voice still hadn't come back yet. It always took longer than I wanted it to before I felt more like myself. At least the shivering had stopped. But the ghastly woman's face wouldn't leave my head. I couldn't focus on anything Daddy was saying to me as he got settled into his seat—something about fear and change and blah blah blah. Only that whisper, that terrible way she'd croaked out *home*, was on my mind.

". . . But if you think you'll be okay here, I'll feel better about seeing you off. So you think you'll be okay?"

I had no clue what he was saying before that. But his eyes were heavy with worry and I didn't want to disappoint him. I nodded, and he sighed in relief.

"Good," he said, tapping both hands on his steering wheel. "So you're gonna try and have a good time here? It's only for a semester. We just need a few months to get MawMaw Septine's affairs in order, and I know Louisiana makes you itchy."

His normal laugh came out, deep and husky and warm like a hug. It made me smile.

"And!" Daddy lifted his hands for emphasis. "Guess what? Auntie Nooncie transferred here just for you, so you'll be less alone! Surprise!"

"Seriously? *Just* for me?"

"Well, also it's more money than her last teaching gig. But still!"

Daddy looked about as excited as I felt hearing that. Nooncie Burton was Daddy's homegirl growing up, as he would say just to make me and Egypt cringe. He'd told me about some trouble they'd get into now and then. And she showed up to family functions like she was blood related. I'd have to call her Miss Noon and not Auntie Nooncie, probably, but that was a small price to pay just to have one of my safe people within the same zip code. I'd have someone who already knew about my autism.

"Thank you," I said, finding myself smiling even more. "Fries?"

"Sure thing, boss," he said while starting up the creaky old Toyota that he refused to trade in.

I breathed deep and looked back toward the school one more time—and all the warmth I felt from our conversation drained away. Immediately I screamed.

The ghastly woman stood right outside my window. And she wanted in.

Dirty, jagged fingernails clawed at the glass.

The woman's mouth hung open in a silent wail, wide like a snake about to strike.

I hid my face against my knees while trying to make myself as small as possible. I was about to start yelling all the protective prayers my grandma taught me when I felt a touch against my arm.

"Hey! Hey, what's the problem?" Daddy said.

I couldn't catch my breath. How could he not see—

But when I lifted my head, the ghastly woman wasn't there anymore. I couldn't stop shaking. She had been *right there*, but . . .

"Nothing," I mumbled. My heart crashed around in my rib cage like a cornered cat. Deep breaths, I reminded myself. In and out, a steady rhythm. "Sorry. I'm fine. Everything is fine." Even though it felt anything *but* fine.

CHAPTER 3

When we got back to the school after lunch, Daddy helped me unpack in my new dorm room. I would be living in a stately redbrick building called Clearwater Hall. We didn't speak, and normally that would be okay. But this silence felt different. Like heaviness melted over the room and onto our heads and spilled right down our throats to keep us quiet. Like the room itself demanded our silence.

I wanted to say as much to Daddy. I wanted to tell him about seeing the ghastly woman among the magnolias, and how this dorm room had bad vibes, and how I'd rather be itchy in Louisiana than stay here and run into that woman again.

Not that anything in the room *looked* off—it looked perfectly fine. Like the modest studio apartment I imagined Egypt was living in in New York. Half the room sat blank, a boring showroom, an imagine-yourself-living-here kind of empty. A pair of desks divided the room, set up so that we'd have to look at each other if we used them at the same time. Both sides had full-size beds, and my new roommate had outfitted hers with dark purple sheets and a black comforter. Maybe we'd actually get along.

The wardrobe I was stuck using had a drawer near the bottom that refused to close, even when I slammed my leg into it. I tried a few more times, then gave up. Some of my stuff would have to go into the closet instead. I shivered. The closet was huge, a walk-in that already had clothes hanging on the left. But something about it seemed . . . wrong.

"You got too many clothes, Doods," Daddy commented while tossing a pair of rolled-up socks at me. I batted them away with an annoyed groan, but really I was glad that Daddy managed to get out from under that heaviness enough to talk to me.

"I know," I said. I crammed some of my notebooks into the top drawer of the well-worn desk at the foot of my new bed. "Take it up with Mama."

"Oh, trust me, I have." He laughed before placing my patch-and-button-covered jean jacket on top of my suitcase with a sigh. "I'm a little worried about you," he said. "You seemed real rattled earlier."

"I'm okay," I said a little too quickly.

Daddy raised an eyebrow but didn't comment. Good. I didn't want him to worry even more. Especially if it meant he might tell Mama I was struggling and I'd get shipped off to some specialized school. And that would just stress her out more and add to her grief plate.

I smiled, even though it felt awkward because I didn't particularly feel like it. "I'll be fine," I added. "I just . . . We got separated and I got scared. And then I thought I saw something. But I'm not scared now! I promise. I'll be fine here. If Egypt can handle New York City alone, I can handle this."

"Well. If you're sure." He stood up, grunting like an old man and mumbling something about his knees. "You understand why you gotta stay here for a bit, right?" I nodded. "If you think it might be too much for you, I can withdraw you. Find a closer school. Whatchu think?"

I thought it sounded delightful. Time in Louisiana with Mama and Daddy instead of here in a place I didn't know with a maybe haunted magnolia grove? Obviously I'd take Louisiana. But . . . I liked Mississippi. I liked the thought of wandering through the same halls that Daddy once did; it made things kinda comforting knowing he'd been here and felt safe sticking me here, too. Knowing Auntie Noo—or, rather, Miss Noon—was here helped, too, since I could talk to her about anything. And I really wanted to give living here a chance.

Against my gut, I shook my head. "I want to stay at this

school," I said, trying to sound as convincing as possible. "You went here, and you're cool, I guess. So I wanna go here, too."

Daddy chortled, an honest-to-goodness chortle. He gently tugged some of my braids before poking the tip of my nose. "Okay," he said. "Proud of you, kid."

"Knock, knock!"

Daddy and I both jumped. Miss Pixie stood in the doorway, hands on the shoulders of another girl. The girl had the longest ink-black hair I'd ever seen and big hazel doll eyes with super-long lashes. I wondered if she was wearing mascara. Mama hated describing humans using food colors, always taking the time to tell us that usually only marginalized people got stuck with food skin-tone names, but all I could see when I looked at this girl's scarless skin was salted caramel from this one café in Rome. It had topped the most delicious drink I'd ever had and was this beautiful shade of tan that had burned into my brain. I'd forced my family to get at least one of these frozen drinks each day we vacationed there. I thought about telling all that to my new roommate, but it definitely would've been too weird. For now, at least.

She fussed with the hem of her crow-covered shirt and bit the side of her lip. Nervous habits. Dr. Choudhury would be proud of me for noticing. Watching her fidget made my own fingers twitch. I didn't want to stim in front of this new potential friend, though, so I slipped my hands into my hoodie pocket and wiggled my fingers in secret instead.

"Hope unpacking is going okay," Miss Pixie said. "This lil nugget here is your new roommate."

"I'm Vee," the girl said. "Hi."

I forgot for a minute that I was supposed to say something back. But I searched my mental cue cards and put on a smile. "Hi, Vee, I'm Eva," I said with a silent prayer that I sounded natural. "Nice to meet you."

"Umm . . . yeah."

Vee looked confused and I grimaced. I must have said something wrong. Maybe it was too formal? I had to remember to soften myself, to not be so stiff and robotic so the other kids would like me.

Miss Pixie ran a hand along Vee's hair, her bright orange acrylic nails standing out against the deep black. "I think you two will get along super well," she said. "If you're hungry, it's almost dinnertime. Sloppy joes tonight!"

"They're probably not gonna be good," Vee said. She smiled at me, but without showing her teeth. That made it tough to decide if it was sincere or not. First on my stay-at-Blythe agenda—befriend Vee.

"Oh, now, don't say that!" Miss Pixie insisted. "Ami's a good cook . . . sometimes." She patted Vee's shoulders and pushed her forward a little. "Anyway, a few quick things for you, Dad, that I'll talk to Eva about more in depth once she's settled. I'm the resident assistant for Clearwater Hall, so if you need anything or you get antsy and want to know how Eva's doing without calling her directly, just call me up instead. Okay?"

"Sure," Daddy said as he nodded.

"And if we need anything, like there's an emergency or Eva gets sick, we'll call you," Miss Pixie continued. "But we probably won't have to do that."

"Great, great," Daddy said. He squeezed my knee but I didn't feel very comforted by it. "All right, Doodles. I'm out for now, but I'll see you in a few days, yeah? Gotta box up the last few things and then I'm off to Louisiana. You ready to stay here by yourself?"

I wasn't, but I faked another smile and nodded anyway. Meeting Vee made me feel a little bit less anxious. At least my roommate would be cool. Hopefully. I had to stay to find out.

CHAPTER 4

Vee smelled like sunshine. It might have been her hair, parted in two and braided—she moved her head a lot as we walked and I caught a whiff of that warm, clean smell with each step. I thought about asking but held it in; commenting on how someone smelled seemed too weird for a first impression. It could wait until next week, or maybe the week after. People liked compliments, and it would help with the befriend-Vee mission.

She shared little details about herself as we walked to the dining hall and I repeated them in my head so that I could remember. Her family came from the Dominican Republic, she said, and she attended Blythe on a scholarship. She had three brothers, all older, but only one she actually liked. She wanted to be a vegetarian, but cheeseburgers tasted too good. Last summer, she got her ears pierced for a second time and one day she wanted to have her whole lobe covered in piercings. We would be good friends, I thought as she rambled, as long as I kept up my "normal human girl" mask.

"I make good burgers," she said. "Friday's my kitchen assistant day so you'll get to taste 'em then. Unless you're a vegetarian. Or vegan."

"I'm not," I said.

The dining hall stood squat against the landscape, surrounded by dozens of magnolias wavering in the warm October wind. Weathered stone walls, rustic roof, huge windows. The dining hall lacked the weird vibes of the dorm and I was more than glad to spend time here and away from the room. Some older girls walking way too close together nudged past us to go in. My heart sped up with this new reality. I needed to be social. Around strangers. Alone.

I wanted to cry. Again.

But I held it in, smiled now and then at other students we passed. I expected the inside to look like a cafeteria, but it was more like a huge home kitchen and dining room combination. A couple of adults and one girl about my age danced around the kitchen and each other as they prepared food. Whiffs of garlic, pepper, tomato sauce, other warm spices I couldn't really place floated through the air. It smelled delicious, but I reminded myself to not get my hopes up; this kid wasn't a good cook, according to Vee. And I knew it was more than likely that I might not like anything, anyway, thanks to my food aversions. The cereal bar in my pocket was likely to become my dinner.

Vee whistled three quick, sharp notes, and the girl in the kitchen looked toward us. She grinned and waved before gesturing to the sauce-covered spoon in her hand. I expected Vee to ditch me. Instead, she took hold of my wrist and tugged me along. My skin crawled—I *hated* being touched at random, especially by strangers or anyone outside my safe person list. But I held my complaints in and tagged along for the sake of my stay-at-Blythe mission.

"This is my new roommate," Vee said as she tilted her head toward me. "Eva. She's in our grade. Eva, Ami. They're weird."

"I'm fabulous," Ami said with a flip of their frizzy dark hair. They grinned at me and their catlike brown eyes sparkled. "Man, am I glad you're here, new roommate Eva."

It wasn't what I was expecting. They were supposed to start with something like, *Where are you from?* or *How do you like Blythe so far?* I had to shift my mental script to go along with this change.

"Why? I didn't do anything," I said.

Ami's upturned nose crinkled as they laughed. "You're Black," she said. "Right?"

"Right."

"So, you did *that*." She nodded. "I was getting kind of bored of being one of only, like, three Black girls in our grade. There used to be Kiana Sallis, but she moved away in fourth grade, so it's been just me and Vee. And Theo Waters, but she doesn't even acknowledge I exist, so I don't acknowledge her, either. And half the school says I don't *really* count as Black, anyway, because my mom's Thai. Which is stupid. I'm Black *and* Thai, y'know? I contain multitudes."

Ami puffed their chest out. A quick glance to their denim vest revealed bunches of buttons and enamel pins—a pronoun button that said *they/them*, lots of cute characters from a show I only sort of knew about, lots of feminism, lots of Black pride. It made me think of Daddy giving his mom's Black Panther beret to Egypt this summer and all the pins attached to it, and Daddy explaining the significance of them to us both. Hope bloomed in my chest—I could *definitely* be friends with Ami.

But I didn't know how to respond to their comment; it would take a few conversations before I could figure out how exactly the flow of chatting worked with them. I hoped I'd get the chance to learn. Fortunately for me, Vee laughed and spoke so I didn't have to.

"They think I don't count, either," Vee said. "Afro-Latina is still Black, y'know?"

"We go to school with a bunch of cretins," Ami said to me. They leaned in like it was a secret, gesturing their spoon at me before winking.

I had no idea what a cretin was, but I nodded anyway. Vee had a light complexion, but Ami had skin closer to mine. Ami was shorter than me, though, and thinner. Their face begged to be drawn, and my hand flexed almost instinctively. I hadn't gotten the urge to draw lately, and it had started to bug me. But Ami's face seemed ready to break my artist's block.

Too much time had passed and I hadn't said anything else in the conversation. I tried to bring myself back, to stop staring at their features to memorize them and actually look them in the eyes. But not in a creepy way, Dr. Choudhury would have reminded me. A friendly way. A soft way.

"I think you'll like it here, new roommate Eva," Ami said. They stopped stirring the saucy meat in the skillet and cut off the burner of the stove. "And if you ever get tired of Vee, I'm right down the hall from y'all. Room 212. Knock anytime."

"Okay," I said. "Um . . . thank you." Were they just being nice? Or did they actually mean it? I wanted them to want to be my friend for real, but I'd learned that people don't always say what they mean.

"No prob." Another smile and wink, and then Ami whirled away toward some cabinets behind them.

"I'm gonna go wash my hands," Vee said.

I started to volunteer myself to join her, just so I could have something to do, when I remembered I'd forgotten my ADHD and antianxiety meds in the dorms. She had already started off before I could ask her to walk back to our room with me. Anxiety bubbled in my stomach, right along with a familiar hungry grumble. Shouting for her to wait was out of the question, and so she got smaller and smaller until she disappeared through a set of double doors.

Ami busied themself with serving kids who had lined up for the meal. Walking back alone appealed to me about as much as eating spoonfuls of sea salt, but I didn't have a choice. With a deep inhale, I spun around to head for Clearwater.

As soon as I stepped forward, I bowled right into another person, knocking myself over. My elbow hit the hardwood floor before the rest of me did and I winced in pain. Something hot soaked into my shirt and I did my best not to cry at the sting.

"Jeez! Watch where you're going!" The girl I'd collided with spoke shrilly. I winced. I hated making people angry, hated being spoken to like I was an idiot. That tone made it impossible for me to look up at her, so I stared at her shoes instead to try and center myself.

Her shoes, from my viewpoint on the ground, cost more than my entire outfit. Egypt had had a picture of the same shoes, bright purple and velvety with a silver buckle and short stacked heel, taped to her vanity for weeks this summer. She'd begged Daddy for an advance on her allowance to get them, but he'd joked that he didn't have that kind of money to give. So this girl was either very rich or very lucky.

"Sorry," I said. I kept my voice low. If I'd learned anything from being the new kid so many times, it was that making enemies so soon was a no-no.

This girl's outfit looked designer, too, I noticed from a quick glance up. She had thin black-framed glasses and a bunch of raspberry-tinted gloss and her small round nose had iridescent highlighter on it. Her hair looked smooth, too perfect, like a wig I might've seen on an auntie at MawMaw Septine's church. Mama would *never* let me straighten my hair this way, but for a second I really wanted to. And to top it all off, even though we were about the same skin tone, her limbs weren't speckled with chicken pox scars and the memories of reckless summer fun like mine. She was beautiful, and she already hated me.

CHAPTER 5

As I hurried back to my dorm, embarrassment pushed me to decide to eat my cereal bar dinner in my room instead of going back out. Besides, the sun was sliding behind the trees, and I had no desire to run into the ghastly woman once the light was gone. But really, I felt a little more nervous to run into that ridiculously pretty girl again. My brain attempted to fixate on the possibility of seeing her, of doing something so cool to make up for the collision earlier that she'd immediately like me. It was never going to happen, so I shifted my focus onto singing my favorite Karen Cooper song to myself. They were my favorite band, and the fast tempo really helped my hustle. I reached the dorm in no time.

Some other girls were waiting for the elevator, so I took the stairs instead. This was a terrible time to try and make friends. My head was swimming too much to pretend to be like everyone else.

When I reached 218, I made myself stop and take a few more deep breaths. I'd made it to my room without seeing anything creepy or running into anyone else. I was okay. I just needed to change my shirt and take my meds and everything would be fine. I wouldn't go back to the dining hall today, but other than that, totally fine.

This time, the heavy doors of the wardrobe refused to open. I really wanted to hit it, but breaking my wrist wasn't on my agenda. Growling at it had to do. I plopped down in my desk chair and rubbed at my eyes. They stung, mostly out of frustration and embarrassment. But also because I missed my family. Just a couple of hours of independence and I already couldn't handle it.

"Get a grip, Eva," I muttered.

A short creak answered me.

Immediately, I tensed. Vee hadn't come back to the room; I sat alone. Maybe the noise was the building settling? I'd read on the school website that Clearwater was built in 1945, so being almost a hundred years old probably meant it shifted and groaned in the same way older people did. MawMaw Septine's house, the one in New Orleans Mama and Daddy had to clear out, often made creepy noises because of its age. Old house sounds happened all the time.

Creeeeeeeaaaaaaaaaaaaaaaaaaaakkkkkkkk.

A longer, lower noise this time, and the hair on my arms prickled up. I didn't want to move, but I didn't want to stick around, either. From the corner of my eye, I watched the closet door slowly, slowly, slowly creep open. It stopped seconds later, and so did my heart. The floor seemed level and the room had no drafts—so why was the door opening?

"I'm just going to change my shirt," I said. "I'm not here to bother anybody. So I'd appreciate if you didn't bother me."

Logically, I knew better than to think something—or someone—lurked in the closet. But logic and cultural beliefs didn't always play well together, like Mama would say. And the superstitions from Mama's side of the family were embedded in me. If something hung around in this room, I needed to be polite, respectful, and clear about my intentions. And all I intended was to eat my sad snack-dinner and go to sleep.

I still couldn't get the wardrobe open after tugging on it again. The rest of my clothes hung in the closet. Because of course they did. I stared at the open closet door. My shirt was still damp and it bugged my sensory sensitivities, but . . . maybe I could suck it up for now. At least until Vee came back to the room.

A *click* from the closet took my breath away. Not even a second later, the light in the closet turned on. My feet carried me out of my room and into the hallway before my brain even processed that I wanted to run.

The bathroom wasn't where I intended to go, but it *was* where I wound up. Most of the part of the bathroom I could see looked pretty clean, although a set of cubbies fully packed with overflowing shower caddies lined the right wall. Beside them, a little red velvet love seat with patches balding from wear sat opposite a long counter with three fancy sinks and a massive mirror with bright vanity lights.

Another door stood just beyond the sinks, and after knocking and waiting, it felt safe to peek and check out what lay behind that second door. To the right, a huge white porcelain tub, the kind with those lion paws holding it up, and a big saucer-like showerhead. A smaller sink and a toilet were straight ahead, with a big shelving unit filled with towels, washcloths, and more to the left.

On the positive side, it felt like a real at-home bathroom, which was way easier to deal with than some airport-style wall of stalls designed specifically to torture me. And my curiosity about the bathroom briefly made me forget about the noise in my room. But the second I thought about it again, my heart sped up. The bathroom suddenly seemed like the worst choice I could've made when trying to hide from whatever I'd heard. At any second I could easily be cornered and trapped in here. Calming myself seemed to be failing.

I backed away from the interior door and turned to the sinks. I switched on the cold water and cupped my hands to splash my face. Cold water helped calm people sometimes, I'd learned, and I needed all the calm I could get. Having my face wet bugged me almost as much as wet clothes, but it felt necessary. I'd experienced too much stimulation too quickly, and a huge chunk of it was too creepy. I tried some self-soothing stimming, swaying in place, and started to mumble another Karen Cooper song to feel better. I turned the water off, swiped droplets from my face, and straightened back up.

Only, when I looked into the huge mirror, I wasn't standing alone.

My first thought: The ghost or spirit or whatever from my room had followed me into the bathroom. This ghost, unlike the woman in the trees, was just a kid like me—barely shorter, about my complexion, a blank, almost sad expression. She spoke up before I had time to form a second thought.

"Did you forget how to drink?" she joked, folding her arms over her chest. "It goes in your mouth, not on your clothes."

"I bumped into someone," I said. Okay, she was a little rude, but at least she was real, not a ghost. I watched her through the mirror, as if looking over at her actual self might make her disappear. "Sorry, I'll go."

"You don't have to," the girl said. "I haven't seen you here before."

"It's my first day," I said.

31

Something crossed her face that I didn't recognize. She smiled like I'd just reminded her of an inside joke. I got the feeling I didn't want to know the punch line.

"I'm Mac," she said. "Nice necklace."

Mac didn't look too fancy or polished. Her high-top sneakers were well-worn and the rubber trim was peeling away from the canvas upper part. She wore jeans smudged with grease or black paint or something and a plain white shirt. Her hair, the long curly fluff of my dreams, was gathered behind her in a low ponytail. She looked nice enough, but I still wasn't feeling very social.

"Thank you . . . I'm Eva," I said as I instinctively clutched my locket. I paused and finally looked away from the mirror to look directly at her. "Nice to meet you."

"Likewise. Welcome to Blythe." Mac spoke with a small lisp, and I could see a small gap between her teeth as she smiled. "We're going to be good friends."

"We are?" Her comment warmed me. I believed her when she said that; something about her felt like she wouldn't say that to just anyone. And for whatever reason, I felt glad she'd chosen to say it to me.

A tinkling melody started to play, and I looked around to try and find the source.

"What's that?"

"The curfew bell," Mac said. "Lucky for you, you're already home."

She gestured for me to walk out first. For a second, I thought she might try and prank me—sticking a sign to my back or yanking my pants down or putting gum or bugs in my hair. But those things happened more in movies, not in real life. I'd never gotten hair-spidered before. No sense stressing about it now.

As fate would have it, I once again found myself face-to-face with the pretty girl from the dining hall. She'd changed clothes, unlike me, but judging by her glossy snarl she wasn't ready to forgive me. Making enemies directly countered my mission to stay here and stay under the radar. So I smiled as warmly as I could.

"We meet again," I joked. Or, tried to. She didn't laugh. "Sorry about bumping into you earlier. I'm Eva."

"I don't care," she said. "Stay out of my way."

Her shoulder smashed into mine as she moved past me. I sighed. My brain already latched on to this girl, and I needed to change her mind about me.

But before that, I needed to survive my first night in my creepy room.

CHAPTER 6

I slept without dreaming. Strange, since most of the time, I had weird dreams—nightmares, even—in places I'd never slept before. But I'd gotten help from Vee to fix my wardrobe, I'd changed into some pajamas, I'd laid my head down, and the next thing I knew, morning had arrived with the gentle chime of Vee's alarm.

Comparing our schedules, Vee wasn't in my homeroom, and we wouldn't have any classes together until the afternoon. But she invited me to sit with her and Ami and a few other kids at breakfast so I didn't have to sit alone. Even so, nerves made it hard to eat, though the fluffy pancakes, cheesy scrambled eggs, maple sausage links, and biscuits and gravy smelled amazing. I managed to eat half my biscuit and drink some grape juice before starting toward homeroom.

Lucky for me, Ami *was* in the same homeroom and, even better, I had been placed in Auntie Nooncie's class. *Miss Noon.* I repeated it in my head a few times to make sure I remembered to call her the right name.

I didn't have to struggle to find the right building or the right room since Ami and I walked together. It felt surprisingly normal to stroll to class and chat with them, even though I snuck furtive glances at the creepy trees on our walk. I thought about asking Ami if they got weird vibes from the woods, too, but that didn't seem like a thing to bring up so soon if I wanted them to like me. I'd have to figure out their stance on spooky supernatural stuff first.

With Ami at my side, no one noticed or cared about me being new. Miss Noon's classroom was decorated exactly how I imagined. Gently encouraging posters dotted the walls, some in Spanish, some in English. Lots of warm colors, browns and peaches and pastel pinks. Her desk had a floppy black corduroy purse sitting on top, but she wasn't in the room. Daddy always teased her a lot about forgetting things or leaving things in random places, so an unattended bag didn't surprise me.

"So, you've gone to school here for a long time?" I asked as I took a seat near the front. Ami stopped, grabbed my backpack, and carried it toward the back.

"Unfortunately," they said, sighing dramatically. They dropped my bag next to a seat in the second-to-last row before plopping down in the seat behind. I took the hint—instead of my typical up-front seat, I moved to sit where Ami placed me.

"Do you like it?" I pulled my hands into the sleeves of my Karen Cooper tour crewneck; it wasn't terribly cold outside, but this classroom may as well have been an icebox. I regretted not grabbing my jacket.

"It's okay," Ami said. "There's a lot of really annoying people." Their gaze drifted, and I turned to follow their line of sight straight to the doorway. In walked the beautiful girl who hated me. My cheeks started to heat up. "But mostly people are chill."

I gave a small wave, but she still must have been mad about yesterday, because she stared me down like she wanted to put thumbtacks in my lunch. I sighed and reached into my bag. Mama had replaced my old, tatty, rubber-band-rigged sketchbook with this shiny new purple glitter one in an attempt to jumpstart my passion for drawing. Even though I'd picked it out myself, I still wasn't comfortable with it and hadn't drawn a single thing yet. But at least staring at the cover kinda took the sting out of the beautiful girl's rejection.

Kids like her didn't need a reason to snap at kids like me, but I certainly wasn't gonna pour extra fuel onto her fire. And besides, as goose bumps crept up my arms, I was becoming way more concerned about how frigid the room felt. Weird, since Miss Noon notoriously considered a balmy seventy degrees to be a little chilly.

"What about the teachers?" I asked. My pencil scribbled aimlessly around the page as I silently wished for some inspiration;

I missed drawing so deeply that my bones ached for it, but I just couldn't start again. "Are they . . . chill?"

"Some of them," Ami said, shrugging. "Most everybody for our grade is cool. Except maybe Mr. Low, the PE coach. He can be a jerk. Oh, and the headmaster. Miss Alice could scare the daylights out of a ghost. But as long as you don't do anything bad, you probably won't get sent to her office."

"Good morning, good morning!" Miss Noon strolled into the classroom just a few seconds before a tinkly little ditty chimed from the black speaker mounted above the whiteboard. She paused at her desk, stuck her bag on the floor, then faced us as she leaned against the edge of the desk. Her voice was one of my favorites of all time, and hearing it gave me a break from worrying about, well, everything. It was soft, almost songlike.

I smiled a little, but kept it to myself. I knew better than to out myself as a potential teacher's pet right off the bat. That kind of information may as well have been a giant PLEASE MAKE FUN OF ME tattoo on my forehead. And I never wanted any tattoos at all.

Today she'd kept her look simple—black capris, ballet flats with gold-capped toes, and a loose-fitting gray cardigan over a white shirt. She'd gathered her thick dark hair up in a high ponytail that cascaded over her shoulder. A very Latina Audrey Hepburn vibe, Egypt would say.

She crossed her tan legs at the ankle and her big brown doe eyes scanned the room. I looked around, too, half to see the other kids around me and half to avoid locking eyes with her.

Most of the desks in the room were occupied. Kids playing on their phones or excitedly whispering or staring outside, probably longing for freedom. Or dreaming of splashing around in the rushing waterfall and stream that I knew was less than a mile away.

A speaker creaked to life overhead to give us the announcements. A voice that somehow managed to be deep *and* nasally gave updates on what to expect for lunch and about where different clubs would be meeting. I looked forward again, and Miss Noon was grinning at me. She gave a tiny flap of her fingers to greet me, and I slumped down with a quiet groan. She was going to make it *way* too obvious that we already knew each other.

She took attendance quickly once the overhead announcements ended. Most of the names I didn't remember, but I was careful to catch the beautiful girl's name—Theo Waters. Even her *name* was pretty. That made her hating me even worse somehow. I had to cut this fixation spiral off before it consumed my brain.

Miss Noon waved to summon me forward. I wanted to shrink down even more. Instead, I got up and trudged toward her desk, and she pulled me closer and shifted me so that I faced the class.

"So, we have a newbie today, as you've likely noticed," Miss Noon said. She clapped her hands against my shoulders. "Class, welcome Eva Mauberry. She just moved here from Tennessee!"

The class buzzed with half-sincere greetings. Even though only a few people even looked up at me, my face burned in embarrassment.

"Eva, anything you want the class to know?"

I knew Miss Noon meant well. But I only knew that because I'd known her since practically before I was born. I carefully tapped my fingertips inside my sleeves and hoped no one noticed the movement.

"I . . . like Karen Cooper?" It was all I could think to blurt out, and only because the front of my shirt caught my focus for a second. "I've seen them live seven times. Once in Germany."

Some of the rumbles from the other kids sounded impressed, and more of the others actually looked at me. Even Theo took a break from scrolling her phone to eye me. I didn't want to jump to conclusions, but it clearly meant she knew my favorite band. Maybe we'd actually have something in common.

But then the girl behind her tapped her shoulder, whispered something as she looked toward me, and they both laughed. My heart sank; suddenly dealing with the ghastly woman felt almost tolerable compared to this.

CHAPTER 7

Nothing anyone said as I sulked back to my desk reached me. All I could think about was Theo laughing at me. Ami mentioned yesterday that she wasn't very nice, but now I knew for certain. As much as I wanted her to like me, I hadn't done anything to deserve being laughed at.

"Did you live in Germany?" Ami asked while I sat back down. "Or is this, like, a rich-kid flex where you went to Germany just for a concert?"

I didn't want to talk. But I also didn't want to fail at my friendship mission. "Lived there," I mumbled. "For a few months . . . for my mom's job."

"Cool." Ami smiled. "Vee's into KC, too. I tried but, I dunno. I like some songs, though. And they're all super pretty—"

I really wanted to focus on what Ami was telling me. But I just kept replaying Theo laughing at me in my head. I stared out the window at a thicket of trees. Not even three seconds later, dark shadows floated among the magnolias. I blinked a few times. As quickly as I'd seen them, they were gone.

I glanced around, but no one else had noticed anything weird. Now that the announcements were done, Miss Noon was at her desk, fiddling with her computer. Everyone else was just waiting for the bell to ring to send us to our first real class of the day.

"Have you ever seen anything weird here?" I asked. Ami looked understandably confused.

"Uh . . . lots," they said. "One time a senior streaked across—"

"No, I mean like . . . spooky weird," I said. "Like . . . something that shouldn't be there."

Ami said nothing, at least not out loud. But their eyes got this drifting look, like they'd gone somewhere else in their head. Like there was something they didn't want to talk about.

"Sounds like the new girl saw the ghost," a boy to the right of us said.

I didn't like his face. He pinched his features all up like a shrew and his breakfast stained his mouth an unflattering brown. And I didn't like the idea of seeing ghosts, either. But the mention of it caught a lot of attention, and some other kids soon joined the conversation. Even Theo turned in her seat a little.

"Are we talking about the ghost?" another voice chimed in from the front.

"Which one?" Someone to my left this time.

"We shouldn't even talk about them. They might show up."

"Joke's on you—they're already here."

The classroom buzzed with excitement, and maybe a little fear. I looked to Ami to see what they thought of this ghost business. They blinked, then looked down at their chipped blue nail polish.

"Is there really a ghost?" I asked. The silence I got after that question felt like an answer. My skin prickled. "Ami, is—"

"There's lots of ghosts," the stain-faced boy said. "You don't know about the accident?"

"Accident?" This was getting worse and worse.

Several people spoke up at the same time, and I squinted. Too much talking at once made my ears hurt, and I desperately wanted to put my headphones on. But I couldn't just be rude and drown everyone out, so I took deep breaths and tried to calm myself.

"I'll tell you," Ami said. They stretched, like telling the story would be a workout. I leaned in automatically.

The legend of Blythe Academy felt more like something from a movie than anything that could happen in real life. The people that bought the land they would eventually build the school on called themselves the Friends of Lafayette Falls Lake, after the waterfall about a half mile away. The area around the falls had

42

already been settled by Black sharecroppers, but the Friends bought their land out and the sharecroppers had to move away.

I'd heard of sharecroppers before; Egypt had done a project on sharecropping last year and I'd listened to her practice presenting it about fifty 'leven times. After the Civil War, once slavery was outlawed, plantation owners still needed labor but didn't have any intentions of having to pay for it. Instead, they'd offer newly freed Black people plots of land to tend—but with a catch, because there's always a catch. The Black people didn't reap the rewards for their work—the landowners got rich instead and left the Black workers with little to nothing to their names. In a fair world, Black people would've been able to build their own wealth and fully own the land. But fairness didn't have a place in oppression, and sharecropping seemed to me like slavery with a fancier name.

Records didn't say what the Friends originally used the land for after their purchase. Eventually, almost a hundred years ago, they opened the school and called it Blythe Academy. According to journals from students back then, the place was haunted from early on. Lots of strange noises, lights flickering, smells of smoke and mold, shadow sightings. And fifty years ago, a huge accident happened. A storm came through, probably the edges of a hurricane. Thanks to some cost cutting during construction, the whole foundation was weak. And to top it off, the land beneath grew too saturated with rain, causing a mudslide. The right side of the building collapsed. A whole classroom of kids and their teacher died.

After the collapse, the hauntings got more intense. They repaired the foundation little by little for years, because they didn't want to close the school down completely. Even after the repairs were done and the building was rebuilt, no one could forget what happened . . . not with the ghosts getting more brazen. Students' things went missing. People felt hands on them. And sometimes, someone would say they saw *her*. The ghastly woman.

They didn't call her by that name, but it had to be the same woman I'd seen in the trees. Tall, wet, decaying—that was my ghost.

Ghost.

I got a little lightheaded just thinking about her.

"But nobody's seen her outside, far as I know," the stain-faced boy said. "That's bananas."

Ami looked at me with what looked like sympathy, but I didn't know if I was reading too much into it.

How long was homeroom supposed to last? Shouldn't the bell have rung by now? Maybe it was just the story getting to me, but being in that room made me feel uneasy. Like I wasn't meant to be in there. Like *none* of us should have been. My classmates didn't seem bothered at all. By now most of them had moved on from the story and were chatting or working on their homework, but I couldn't relax. I took a deep breath, and when I exhaled, my breath was a puff of white.

My skin prickled. It was so cold, like I'd suddenly been teleported to a walk-in freezer. It had been chilly before, but this made no sense. Looking around, I noticed no one else's breath was visible. Nobody else had goose bumps. But I was shivering.

In fact, no one else was moving. At all.

Everyone except for me sat frozen, unblinking, not breathing.

I started to panic. Something was wrong with this room. And that something seemed way too eager to let me know it was there.

Before I could fully freak out, the bell chimed, signaling it was time for the first class of the day. All of a sudden, the other students unfroze and hustled off to class like nothing had happened. And I kind of wondered if maybe nothing *had* happened. Could I have imagined that?

I took my time packing my sketchbook away. Ami kept talking, but none of what they said registered until they mentioned heading off to history.

"Wait!" I surprised myself *and* Ami by calling out. I guess they had gotten used to me being quiet. They turned to look at me with a question in their eyes. "What part of the building collapsed? Like, what room is it now?"

A slow grin unrolled on their face and I instantly regretted asking. "Room 23-B," Ami said before jogging out of the classroom.

My stomach sank and my mouth went dry. Room 23-B. The haunted room.

Our homeroom. *This* room.

CHAPTER 8

I got lost almost immediately trying to find the physical science lab. There weren't any helpful arrows or signs, and I wound up walking in a giant circle. I ended up right back where I'd started, right within the newer section of the building. The section, I knew now, where the accident had happened. I shuddered.

A second bell chimed, and I sighed. I was late. And I still had no idea where the right room was. But homeroom was just a few steps away, and I knew I could talk to Miss Noon without feeling weird.

The door was open just a sliver, and when I peeked through I didn't see anyone. I nudged the door open and slowly slipped inside.

Hints of vanilla and spice wrapped around me now that I was calm enough to notice. It felt like standing inside a tin of Christmas cookies. I breathed in deep and closed my eyes, thinking of all the holidays we'd spent with MawMaw Septine.

She was my mom's mom, and she made Christmas cookies every holiday that smelled kind of like this. We didn't get to go to Louisiana last winter because Mama's videography job had been too far away to afford plane tickets, and I suddenly felt overwhelmingly sad about not getting to say goodbye to MawMaw before her passing.

Miss Noon wasn't here.

My brain cartwheeled down a path of worst-case scenarios: She'd gotten snatched by the ghastly woman and dragged into the trees, or a phantom mudslide had formed and she'd been swallowed by it, or possibly some other ghost—or *lots* of ghosts—had her held captive on the ceiling and kept her from speaking and I'd only discover it when a single tear fell onto the back of my neck.

I couldn't stop myself from a quick glance up. Luckily, no ghostly hands or a terrified Miss Noon. But the silence started to creak to life, and I backed out of the room before I found myself in the company of phantoms.

Nerves made me tap my index and middle fingers to my thumbs while I hustled toward the main office. Not a single student roamed through the halls, and that raised my inner alarms even further. I felt that noisy silence stroll along behind me, almost mocking me, getting closer and closer and closer until at the last second I screwed my eyes shut and threw myself through the office door. Any second, an office worker would yell at me for making a commotion.

Any second.

. . . Any second?

When I opened my eyes, dread stole my breath. The entire office was as empty as the halls had been. No secretary with the red glasses, no queasy kids waiting for someone to take them home, nothing. There could be any number of perfectly reasonable explanations, but the feeling of unease made everything feel creepy.

I dropped my bag down and plopped into a seat. If I waited long enough, someone was bound to come back in. They could help me find my next class, and hopefully help me switch homerooms. Miss Noon was a safe person, guaranteed not to belittle me or decide I was trouble, but there's no way I could go back to her homeroom, as much as I loved her.

A few deep breaths and some leg pat stimming later, I felt slightly calmer. The patting took the nervous energy piling up inside me and let it filter out. Like releasing the valve of a pressure cooker so it doesn't explode. I pulled my sketchbook from my bag and started to sketch.

Drawing made me feel safe, and I was good at it. Daddy often said I did the electric slide out of the womb with a sketchbook and a pair of headphones. I couldn't remember a single day that

I didn't draw, up until MawMaw Septine's passing. And even though I tried to play it cool earlier, my heart was beating two hundred times too fast. Being the new kid sucked. Being the new kid stuck in a ghost warehouse all alone felt worse.

Ten minutes had passed and still no one came in.

But for a second, just a second, I thought I heard a sigh.

Tingling prickled my skin and gave me goose bumps. I held my breath just to make sure I hadn't been the one to make the noise. A few seconds later, it happened again.

"No way," I said to myself.

In our first therapy session together, Dr. Choudhury taught me how to slow down, breathe, assess a situation. And in this situation, I needed to go through all the logical explanations. Sometimes windows had cracks. That would explain a lot of different noises. Or the air conditioning might have kicked on. At our third house last year, the ventilation system sometimes sounded like a startled cat when it started up.

But I couldn't think of anything explainable, hard as I tried, that sounded like *Evaaaaa.*

CHAPTER 9

Whatever was in the office had said my name.

It said my name like a whisper, like trying to get my attention in a dark movie theater.

"You can't hurt me," I said as loudly as I could. My voice shook almost as much as my hands. "Whatever you are, you can't hurt me, and you have no power over me."

That was what MawMaw Septine and Mama told me to tell anything scary. A long time ago, during our last visit before he died, PawPaw Thibodeaux scared the elements outta me with a ghost story from his childhood. He told Egypt and me about being chased by a phantom dog, and I became convinced I'd wind up hounded in the same way one day. I cried about it for almost an hour. But MawMaw Septine and Mama soothed me, explaining that ghosts couldn't do anything to living bodies, and that they especially couldn't do anything if you expressly told them to kick rocks.

I hoped ghosts in Mississippi followed the same set of rules.

I crammed my things into my backpack and stood, then made my way toward the door. I wasn't sure where to go if not even the main office was safe, but I couldn't stay here.

A bowl of candy on the corner of the desk caught my attention. A fun-size bag of sour gummies called to me. I needed something to calm my nerves.

I reached out to snag the gummies on my way out, but before I could take anything, a hand grabbed my wrist and squeezed, hard. I tried jerking away, but it was impossible. The grip just tightened.

Patches of gray-green skin flaked up. The mechanics of the hand were on full display. Gnarled tendons. Aged bones. Rotted muscle. Dirt stained the nails, as if whoever this was had clawed out from six feet under. Drips of sewage-smelling liquid plopped onto the floor. Goose bumps rose along my arms again. This wasn't the hand of anyone who'd been alive anytime recently.

My stomach turned upside down. That smell . . .

That smell was going to kill me.

CHAPTER 10

The second I looked up, I regretted it.

There she was again. The ghastly woman—only this time, half her face was rotting off. The flesh strip dangled down to her chest. A worm shimmied its way through her exposed eye socket. Her scalp slid back to reveal the skull beneath. Even with a decent chunk of her face missing, I could see sadness in her.

Mama and MawMaw Septine both swore ghosts couldn't touch you or hurt you. But here the ghastly woman was, bony fingers holding me in place, making my skin crawl. *How?* How could she be touching me?

Her jaw dropped open like she wanted to say something to me. Dirt and dust and little bugs fell out instead of words. The smell of death—stale and damp and suffocating—surrounded me. I frantically swatted at the bugs flitting against my arms.

I slammed my eyes closed. I didn't know how long I was screaming, or how long the ghastly woman had a hold on me, but by the time I felt myself float back into being present, an entirely different woman was touching me. She wasn't rotting or melting or dead. She *was* pretty angry looking, though.

"Eva Mauberry!" she said loudly as she squeezed my shoulders. "Wake up!"

Being touched by people I didn't expressly give consent to touch me got under my skin—being touch averse made surprise hugs or handshakes dang near impossible. And this woman's hands on me so soon after the ghastly woman held on to my wrist felt like glass shards. Everything hurt and everything was too loud and everything was too much and I couldn't stop yelling.

"Eva, what is the *matter* with you!" The woman didn't seem like she really wanted an answer. Instead, she gave my shoulders a small shake, as if that would jolt me into responding to her.

Behind her, a crowd of kids—and a few teachers, too—were peering into the office. They stood there, watching me, and I couldn't stop yelling even though I wanted to. I felt helpless, like the ghastly woman had infected me with something foul that was trying to swallow me whole.

I broke out of the woman's grip and backed myself toward the corner. I bumped into the desk and made the candy bowl fall, and the clatter made my eardrums feel like they were going to burst.

I clapped my hands over my ears and tucked myself down closer to the ground. My headphones were in my backpack, but I couldn't move again to reach for them. At some point, I must have started crying, because when I rested my face against my knees, I felt tears.

All I wanted was all the noise to stop, all the touching to stop, all the whispers to stop. My heart sped up even more. I felt my throat tighten. I was having a full-blown meltdown in public, something I hadn't done since I was four.

Another hand pressed against my shoulder and I jolted. "Stop!" I shrieked, and the hand immediately pulled away.

"I'm sorry! I'm sorry."

That voice was familiar. Miss Noon was squatting down in front of me, hands on her knees. She smiled gently, even though her eyes looked worried.

"I apologize, Eva," she said as I lifted my head completely. "I'm sorry." She turned her head to call out over her shoulder, "She doesn't like being touched."

"Well, I didn't know that," the other woman snapped.

"I actually discussed that with you—"

"Get her up, and get her into my office."

Miss Noon's mouth pinched up. I recognized that—she only made that face when she was trying not to cuss someone out. "Eva, do you think you can stand?" she asked. "We're going to walk to Miss Alice's office. It's only about twenty feet to your right, and then I'll call your dad. Okay? Do you want help up?"

"No," I mumbled. I pulled my hands away from my ears and stood up. Miss Noon did the same.

"What on Earth were you doing in here in the first place?" Miss Alice asked. The kids in the hall got louder, and if there was one facial expression I was familiar with, it was judgment. It was all over their faces. I wanted to sink into the ground like this school had fifty years ago.

"Let's talk in your office," Miss Noon suggested. She almost put a hand on my back to guide me but drew it back when I looked at her.

"I want an answer *now*," Miss Alice insisted.

"Miss Al—"

"No student is to be out of class without express permission via hall pass at any point," Miss Alice continued. "Do you have a pass?" I shook my head. "Not only are you in a place you aren't meant to be, but you're also clearly skipping class!"

The class dismissal chime started as Miss Alice lit into me. I sighed. Kids poured out of their classes and stood around in the hallway to watch my inevitable punishment. We used to joke that Daddy was cursed with bad timing, and apparently it was generational.

"Miss—"

"Miss Noon, please enlighten me as to why you think trespassing and skipping class are excusable offenses."

"She's autistic," Miss Noon whispered. But she wasn't quiet enough, even though I could tell she was trying. Some kids widened their eyes, some whispered even more, some looked confused . . .

And now my secret was out.

My eyes burned. Tears spilled over my cheeks. Now I *definitely* hated Blythe in a bone-deep way.

CHAPTER 11

Miss Alice's office sat off to the side of the main office, and I was instructed to sit on the bench outside it. From this spot, I could see people coming in and out. I could see the secretaries answering phone calls and filing papers. Where were all these people when I needed them? I could see, if I leaned forward, people looking into the office curiously. Like they wanted to get a glimpse of the weird kid who freaked out.

I adjusted my headphones to make sure they were as tight against my ears as they could be. Karen Cooper to the rescue once again, this time my playlist of their loudest, angriest tracks guaranteed to block out any noise—outside *or* in my own head.

I had never been sent to a principal's office before. Despite the blaring music, my mind raced with thoughts of what to expect. She would call my dad. He would come and be disappointed and I would maybe get detention or suspension or something.

I'd flunk out of school and end up in juvenile detention and then prison. My hands started shaking.

Miss Noon sat nearby. Her right leg bounced and she stared ahead. I wanted to comfort her, even if I was the one who was maybe getting expelled. She had always been nice to me. And now my freak-out might get her fired.

I knew I was being unreasonable. I knew all these scenarios were unlikely to happen. But anxiety didn't care much about the likelihood of something happening. And autism made me terrified to break rules, to rock boats. Combined with an imagination constantly on eleven, the smallest things became catastrophic in a matter of seconds.

Even with how stressful that could be, I wasn't embarrassed or upset about being autistic. Not exactly. I was embarrassed by how I sometimes got overwhelmed, about how I couldn't quite control myself as well as I wanted to when a meltdown started. Only one person, five schools ago, ever said anything mean to me about it. And he'd gotten detention for it. The kids who saw me today probably wouldn't spread it around or bully me. But that small chance that they might consumed me.

Listening to Karen Cooper helped a lot. They were my favorite band, all angry drums and feminist lyrics. They were young, too; the oldest—Drysi, the drummer—was nineteen, and their lead singer, Maddi, was the prettiest sixteen-year-old I'd ever seen. Egypt and I listened to Karen Cooper together a lot, and our only major fight was when she won tickets to a KC show and wouldn't take me along. KC comforted me, and sitting there in the office, I needed all the comfort I could get.

Somehow, Miss Noon and I locked eyes. She smiled, tight-lipped and tired. I tried to smile back but I didn't know if the corners of my mouth even lifted. I felt drained; meltdowns always left me tired and kind of floaty. Dissociation. Lucky me.

I watched Miss Noon's lips move, and I reached to pull a headphone cup off my right ear.

"Oh, I'm sorry," Miss Noon said. She brought a hand to her chest. "I was asking you if you needed anything. Water, or a snack, or . . ."

I shook my head. Talking aloud was always a struggle after a meltdown. But I wanted to try. *Needed* to try. And it would certainly be easier with her. "Thank you."

Miss Noon nodded. She had more to say, judging from the way she opened her mouth a few times, but nothing came out. Instead, she gave another small smile and went back to looking ahead.

My father came through the doorway barely five minutes later—I'd gotten through another song and a half of KC. I felt myself smile more naturally and I stood up. I gave him the OK hand signal to let him know I was better before he could ask.

His shoulders relaxed. "Thanks for calling, Nooncie," Daddy said to Miss Noon as she also stood.

"Oh, it's no problem," Miss Noon said. They nearly hugged, but she seemed to think better of doing that at work. "Thank you for coming so quickly. I didn't want Eva to be uncomfortable for too long."

"I really appreciate that," Daddy said. I shifted to be closer to him, to rest my head against his squishy stomach.

I loved both my parents a ton, but Daddy and I had a special kind of bond that I didn't have with anyone else. He got me on a level that the rest of the family sometimes didn't, and we had so many of the same interests that, if not for the fact that I looked like a mini version of his mom, I might have just been a clone of him.

We walked into Miss Alice's office together once the secretary with the red glasses told us to go in. I squeezed Daddy's hand impossibly tight. When he squeezed back, I felt a little of my tension leave. He helped keep me grounded.

"Eva," Miss Alice said. My name felt heavy in her mouth, and I wished to be called literally anything else. I didn't know if she wanted me to respond or if she was just saying it for dramatic effect.

Her office could have been anyone's. Nothing made it personal to her—not a family photo, not a quirky mug, not even a nameplate. Miss Noon seemed scared of her, and I could understand why. Her voice echoed in my head as I sat with Daddy, waiting for her to tell him all the ways that I'd messed up.

I wondered what color her hair was beneath her tightly tied scarf. Given how pale she was, I thought maybe she was blond, or maybe a redhead. Or maybe she'd gone gray already, from stress or age or both. Since Miss Noon and Daddy were both in their thirties, Miss Alice had to be at least sixty. Maybe she was even older than MawMaw Septine was. I glanced at Miss Alice's hands as she clasped them atop her desk; hands give away a lot about age, I had figured out years ago. Her hands showed wrinkles, age spots, knobbly knuckles. Definitely sixty plus.

"Students at Blythe Academy are expected to attend *every* class assigned to them," Miss Alice said. "While I recognize Eva's . . . differences . . . she is no more exempt from this expectation than any other student."

"Of course," Daddy said. "This isn't like Eva, and I'm sure she has a reasonable explanation as to why she missed her class."

I wanted to laugh but didn't want to get into more trouble; he was using his *talking to white people* voice, and that switch always struck me as amusing. When that voice appeared, he would raise his normally smooth, deep voice by an octave, and he'd chop slang out of his vocabulary almost entirely, and he avoided sounding too Southern, even when we were still in the South. Mama explained to me about code-switching some time ago, about how sounding nonthreatening often meant the difference between life and death for Black and brown people. From then, I'd practiced my own code-switch voice, but Egypt always teased me by saying I sounded pretty nonthreatening in the first place.

Miss Alice didn't seem as amused by Daddy's voice as I did. Her mouth puckered, deeper grooves forming around her lips. She looked at me.

"I won't assign a punishment this time," Miss Alice said. "I want you to reflect on the expectations of the academy. Eva, do you understand the seriousness of your behavior? You are not to skip classes, and you are not to traipse into rooms in which you don't belong. Is that clear?"

My throat locked. I still wasn't back to completely normal yet. My gaze moved to Daddy, and he looked back at me with one raised eyebrow. I knew Daddy would speak for me, and he was silently asking if he should, but I really needed to try. At least just to let Dr. Choudhury know I'd made an effort.

But I didn't make an effort. I couldn't explain why I was in the office, or why I wanted to switch homerooms. I nodded again, and I let myself down.

"You're free to go," Miss Alice said. I stood fast enough to almost knock over my chair and hustled into the hall before she could find something else to scold me for.

CHAPTER 12

When I was six, I picked up the special interest of carnivorous and poisonous plants thanks to *Little Shop of Horrors*. Daddy spent hours reading books about oleander and laurel and nightshade to me. We bought a small Venus flytrap for the windowsill of our apartment. I named a fish I had at the time Seymour. And when the botanical garden in the city we used to live in at the time announced it would be installing a poisonous plant exhibit, I made certain that Daddy got us tickets to the opening. We went back to the gardens almost every day until we moved three months later.

The botanical garden near Blythe didn't have any poisonous plants, but at least there were oleander bushes here. Daddy knew this would be a good place to help me calm down.

We sat together on an ironwork bench dedicated to someone who'd probably donated millions of dollars to the botanical society. Daddy bought us hot cocoa and éclairs from the café inside the main building, and I was enjoying a mouthful of both when he finally spoke to me.

"Doodles, I know this is hard," he said. But it was more like a breath. A world-weary sigh, like Mama would say. "I know new places stress you out. But . . . you'll be here for a decent stretch this time, and I really want you to be comfortable. If this school isn't comfortable for you . . ."

I swallowed. He'd figure something else out. Something that would probably put a lot of unnecessary stress on Mama. I stayed quiet.

"You wanna tell me why you skipped class?" he asked when I didn't say anything. "That's not like you, Doods. You love science."

"I got lost." I whispered it. I didn't trust myself enough to say it any louder than that. The full story itched my throat. I took a swig of hot cocoa to try and wash it back down.

"Okay," Daddy said. He nodded. "Okay, lost. I get that. But you should have found a teacher to help you out. Why did—"

"The school's haunted," I said. That wasn't what I meant to say. I meant to say I was too nervous to talk to anyone who wasn't Miss Noon.

Daddy's side of the family had very different views than Mama's on spirits and spirituality in general. He grew up without superstition, without whispered tales of ghostly ships and wailing mothers wandering Earth looking for their lost children. He believed in science, and in nature, and according to him, that didn't leave room for silly things like ghosts.

"Haunted." He said it like he wanted to laugh in my face, and my cheeks got hot.

"I'm not crazy," I said.

He held his cocoa-holding hand up in defense. "I'm not calling you crazy," he said, "and you know I never would. I've heard about the ghosts at Blythe before."

"You have?" My eyes went wide.

"Oh yeah," he said with a nod. "I didn't live in the dorms or anything, but kids from my time here gossiped about the ghosts, too. My folks have lived round here for . . . over a century, probably. Up from New Orleans, thanks to the slave trade. Settled here in Mississippi. Some moved north to Tennessee after getting free, some to Texas, some kept going north—Kansas City, Chicago . . . There's one twig on the tree that's out in California. But the Mississippi foundation, that's still strong. Part of why I wanted to send you to Blythe.

"When I was little, kids would say all kinds of things about Blythe and the ghosts roaming the halls." He let out a spooky wail, wiggling the fingers of one hand in my face. I swatted him away. Normally his silly little moments made me smile, but the last thing I wanted was to laugh about this. "Anyway, that's

66

all they are. Rumors. Everybody likes to say anywhere old is haunted. It's not true, Doods. I didn't see, or hear, or smell anything weird when I went here. I woulda told you if I did."

"I know what I saw and what I heard," I insisted.

"Okay, so . . . I just need to know a little more. What exactly did you see?"

I took a shaky breath. I couldn't bring myself to tell him. I really didn't want to disappoint him, but even more so I didn't want to be disappointed in him for not believing me. So I rambled about general things—the building collapse, the sightings other kids had spoken of. The only personal experience I could share was the closet door creeping open.

He nodded every few words, and he squinted into the distance the way he does when he's thinking something through. Once I stopped talking, he sighed and sat his cocoa down. He passed a hand over his fade that was getting a little longer than he normally kept his hair.

"You have to find someone to tighten that up," I told him, something I'd heard Mama tease him about my whole life.

That made him laugh, and it made *me* feel a little more at ease. He wasn't going to make fun of me for this. He wasn't. Was he?

"It's on my agenda," Daddy said. He turned his head toward me. "Eva . . . Do you think maybe you got scared by Ami's story and spooked yourself?"

"Leading the witness," I said, and he laughed again.

"I regret explaining that phrase to you," he said. He elbowed me gently. "I'm serious, Doodles. You have an amazing, beautiful imagination, but sometimes it leads you down some spooky paths. So maybe that's the case this time. What do you think?"

I thought it sounded ridiculous. I thought he was treating me like a baby. I thought about telling him about the voice that whispered my name, or about the sighs from nowhere, or the gross hand that had taken hold of my wrist.

The hand.

I pushed up my hoodie sleeve just a bit, just enough to get a look, and I almost dropped my éclair. There, right there, right where the woman had grabbed me, my wrist had the faintest trace of a burn mark.

CHAPTER 13

My stomach churned.

The ghastly woman had marked me. For . . . death? Torture? Was she going to eat me like an evil witch in a fairy tale? I found myself growing angry. MawMaw Septine and Mama *swore* ghosts couldn't hurt the living. So why did I have this burn?

"Doods, what happened to your arm?"

I whipped my head up to look at Daddy and quickly slid my sleeve back into place. "I—"

"Did one of the other kids hurt you? Is *that* why you skipped class?" Daddy turned himself toward me more. His eyebrows knit together, and his mouth deepened into a frown. If I could see his eyes behind his mirrored sunglasses, they'd probably be full of concern.

A lie started in my head. I could have told him that yes, some kid at the school did this to me. That it was some kind of hazing thing. But lying about things like this came to me about as naturally as a fish flying a plane.

I shook my head. "It was a ghost," I said.

Daddy's frown turned into a straight line, and he raised an eyebrow. "Eva . . ."

"Please believe me," I said. "I'm not making this up. A ghost grabbed me in the office and I freaked out and then Miss Alice showed up and—"

"Eva." The sigh that followed felt like a kick to the chest. He *was* disappointed. I could feel it. The flowers around us could probably feel it. "I know you felt scared," he said, and the way he enunciated each syllable fueled the anger welling up inside me. "And I know you and your mom like all this spirit stuff. But I need you to tell me that you know that ghosts can't hurt you."

I refused to look at him. Daddy was patronizing me. He didn't believe me, and he was acting like I was an immature, idiotic child for even saying what I said. I balled my left hand up, my nails digging in so hard to my palm that I just knew if I looked, I'd see blood.

"I don't want to continue this conversation," I said as firmly as I could manage.

"Eva Amari."

"We can go now," I said. I kept my tone flat—flatter than usual, since sometimes with my autism I spoke in monotone by default. I needed Daddy to know I was upset. That I wasn't going to tolerate being spoken down to.

His gaze made my skin itch. I popped the last of my éclair in my mouth and folded my arms over my chest. Upset stance. Dr. Choudhury and I worked on being able to recognize if someone was upset a lot.

Daddy hummed and stood, and he slowly walked toward a trash can nearby.

"You are definitely your mother's child," he said. "I apologize for making you feel bad. We don't have to talk about this anymore if you don't feel like I'm hearing you."

"I don't, because you're not." I stood. "Blythe has ghosts. And one of them attacked me. But you don't believe me, so." I shrugged. "I wanna go back to my dorm room now."

I managed to push myself to talk, and what was the point? Daddy didn't believe me. And ghosts at this new school had decided I was some kind of easy target. I wanted to scream, but I was mad at myself, too, for not even being able to do that.

But I would show everyone. I would prove them, and myself, wrong. I had to get proof about the ghosts messing with me, and I had to find a way to share that proof without clamming up.

I headed toward the parking lot, trying to calm all the rage swirling in my stomach. For the first time in my whole life, I couldn't wait for Daddy to leave me behind.

CHAPTER 14

"I believe you," Vee said.

We sat on her bed—the two of us and Ami—after another meal I struggled to eat. Ami laid with their head in Vee's lap while Vee petted their hair. I tried not to stare, but their relationship fascinated and depressed me. I had never had a friend I felt comfortable enough with to lie on, or to have lie on me. Other objectives in my mission would come first, but maybe I could add this goal, too.

"My lala saw ghosts," Vee added. "Before she died, she told us that her husband, my papa, visited her in her room. But *he* died three years before *she* did. Isn't that freaky?"

"Super freaky," Ami agreed. "When I die, you have to come visit me." They reached up and pointed their finger at Vee, and Vee touched her index fingertip to it.

"Deal," Vee said. "Unless you die first. Then you have to come to me."

"I don't think you get to choose," I said. They both looked at me, and I wished I could take it back. Now they would hate me, for sure.

"It's just a fun thought," Ami said. "We're not serious."

"Oh." I paused. "Well . . . Thanks for explaining. I promise I'm not dumb."

"Nobody thinks you're dumb," Vee said as Ami agreed. "I get it. Autism makes you super literal sometimes. Nothing to be sorry for or embarrassed about."

"And if anybody gives you crap about it, tell us," Ami said as they put their feet up on the wall, right on top of Vee's poster of a glittery goth mermaid. "We'll fight. I know tae kwon do."

"Anyway," Vee said, tapping Ami on the head. "We already know the campus is haunted. I don't think it's too weird to think whatever is here showed itself to you. Maybe we should cleanse you."

"Or cleanse the whole dorm," Ami said.

"The whole campus."

They kept one-upping each other with places to cleanse. For a second, I felt awkward. Left out. Joking around with a BFF wasn't something I had any experience in. To keep from fixating on that, I let my mind wander. No one but my sister had ever volunteered to fight anyone for me. And I hadn't been part of a "we" before. My mission to make friends seemed like it was off to a good start so far. But cleansing everything might draw too much attention. That was a no-go. Taking time to clear any bad energy from our room, at least, made sense. And we'd start with the closet.

Almost like it heard my thoughts, the closet door creaked. Ami and Vee quieted down. All of us watched the door, barely breathing. Tension knotted my insides as I waited for it to move again. Ami started to speak, but Vee shushed them.

Nothing happened. The door stayed still, and we all let out a sigh.

Ami sat up and swung their legs over the side of the bed. "Well, curfew soon come," they said in an island-type accent. "I'll see y'all tomorrow."

"I gotta get myself ready for bed," Vee said while getting up, too. "Do you wanna come, Eva? Or will you be okay till I get back?"

I didn't want to sit in here alone. But I also didn't want them to think I was a baby. So I told them I'd be fine. I quietly hoped I wasn't lying.

As soon I was alone, my heartbeat crept faster. My body anticipated something, and I didn't even know what. But that came regularly with anxiety, so I tried not to worry too much. Worry somehow translated to feeling chilly, and I faced a new dilemma. All my hoodies hung in the closet, the last place I wanted to enter. But hoodies also made it easier to disappear into myself when things got overwhelming.

I silently hyped myself up before I dragged my feet to cross the room, slow as I could. Opening the closet door took all my energy. But nothing scary happened. Thank goodness.

My hoodies hung near the back of the closet. Because of course they did. One hoodie, familiar but not my own, caught my attention. It was soft and well-worn with a Coney Island sideshow screen print on the back. Daddy's hoodie.

I nearly cried pulling it from the hanger. Holding it to my face, I counted to ten while breathing in pine and flowery laundry detergent and other things that made up Daddy's scent. Tomorrow he'd be heading out of town, and our last conversation in person was an argument.

My bravery slipped away from me after a few seconds, so I closed the closet door and shuffled toward my bed.

Vee said she would be right back. I just needed to handle a couple more minutes of being alone and then I would be okay. I could ask if she ever had weird feelings in here.

A knock froze me in place. My attention shifted to the bedroom door, but the knock came from somewhere else.

The closet.

Something in the closet was *knocking*.

Cold sweat started to run down my neck. Something knocked in the closet. The *empty* closet. MawMaw Septine taught us that three knocks meant trouble. Three knocks in a row couldn't be anything other than something dark. Something dangerous.

I wondered how close together those three knocks had to be.

"I'm not going to acknowledge that," I said loudly. I uncovered my phone from beneath some discarded pajama pants and cheered in my head. "I'm leaving. Because I don't hear anything."

Knock

Knock

KNOCK

I shrieked and hotfooted my way to the door.

CHAPTER 15

After sitting with Miss Pixie until I was able to calm down—failing, again, to communicate the truth of what had happened—I reluctantly returned to my room. Sleep barely visited me that night. I kept waking up, sweaty and confused and feeling like I was being watched. On top of feeling uneasy, my dreams—nightmares, really—were filled with short flashes of horrible accidents. Flooding, earthquakes, landslides, and screaming that I felt in my bones would stay with me for weeks.

When Vee's alarm went off, I zombie-shambled to the bath-room to get ready for the day. She was nice enough to walk with me to breakfast but left early to go find her history teacher before school started. I could barely eat, so a few minutes later I packed up my things and started to walk to the academic building.

I started to shake; what if the ghastly woman showed up, waiting for me, ready to grab me again?

A hand touched my shoulder and I yelped.

Mac laughed. *"You're* a jumpy Jenny this morning. Too much coffee?"

"I've never had coffee," I said while I adjusted my backpack to hold the straps tighter. "And nobody says 'jumpy Jenny.'"

A word vomit of anxiety about what happened in the classroom, in my dorm, almost came up. But I swallowed it back and slowly started to walk with her. My nerves built with every step. The ghastly woman was going to be there again today. My bones practically vibrated with certainty about it.

"So? Anyway, try coffee. You're missing out," Mac said. "Heard you had an episode in the office. Rough. And on your first day, too."

"I would rather not talk about it," I mumbled.

Mac grew quiet. We walked in step without a word. I almost felt bad about shutting the conversation down. Especially since I really was happy to see her. She had the potential to be the Ami to my Vee. But I couldn't think or talk about the ghost and everyone seeing me freak out. I needed a do-over. A course correction. A way to get back on track and not get sent to a different school.

As we approached the main building for middle schoolers, I noticed a custodian on a stepladder hanging a sign above the main doors. I squinted to make it out.

BLYTHE ACADEMY CENTENNIAL CELEBRATION

COME CELEBRATE THE BIG 1-0-0 WITH US!

OCTOBER 30, 11 a.m.–10 p.m.

ALL AGES!

The fiftieth anniversary was when the building collapsed; for one hundred years, what if something worse happened?

The celebration was about a week away. Would that be enough time to prepare myself for the kind of tragedy that might happen? Another huge storm, maybe. A molasses flood. Alien invasion. An explosion, maybe, or the spirits here possessing everyone on the campus. Maybe even the terrible things I saw in my nightmares. My imagination could barely keep up with itself mulling over all the ways this celebration could go wrong.

I felt a shove, and I was jolted out of my thoughts as I lurched forward. I swiveled to glare at whoever had knocked into me, but it was just Ami. They grinned, full of mischief and teasing.

"Ready for day two?" they asked. They waggled their eyebrows. I thought about asking what that meant but settled on smiling instead.

"I think so," I said. "Oh, do you know Mac?"

"Who?"

"Mac, my friend here—"

But Mac no longer stood at my side. I didn't see her anywhere nearby, either. I frowned. She could have at least said bye before leaving. My stomach turned a little thinking that maybe I really had hurt her feelings. I pinned a mental note to the corkboard in my brain to apologize the next time I saw her.

"Eva!"

Ami and I both turned. Theo stood on a connecting path not far off from us. She held on to her backpack straps as she ran over to us.

"Hey," Theo huffed. She glanced to Ami before talking to me again. "Um. Here."

She pulled her backpack around to her front and rummaged through it. Ami crossed their arms and raised an eyebrow. I'd told Vee and Ami all about Theo being rude, but I didn't expect either of them to care much. "What are you doing?" they asked. "If you're trying to be a jerk again—"

Theo handed me a package of wire-free earbuds. A pink pair, not a color I would have chosen, but . . . I recognized the brand from my almost unending search for the perfect headphones to deal with sensory overload. They were pretty expensive, way more than I would have paid for a gift for a near-stranger. I'd wanted to change her mind about me, but I hadn't actually done anything.

"I heard about what happened. My brother likes using these," Theo said. "Not as obvious, really good noise canceling, studio-quality audio."

". . . Thank you."

No one at any other school had given me a gift before. The surprise and relief felt as comforting as a favorite hoodie.

Ami must have been shocked, too, because they didn't say a word. Instead they took my free hand and pulled me up the stairs before I could say anything else

"Don't trust her," they said. "She's not nice. For all we know, those headphones are bugged so she can spy on you for some kind of trick."

I looked over my shoulder. Theo still stood beneath the banner. And she was looking at me, too. I watched her smile, watched her wave just barely before a friend grabbed her attention. Even with Ami's warning, my heart thumped a little harder as I waved back.

CHAPTER 16

Ami went right into homeroom, but I hesitated in the doorway and backed out. I needed some time to gather my wits in the bathroom. Sometimes I needed to go over affirmations in the mirror like Dr. Choudhury taught me. It helped make me more confident and less anxious. So maybe it would help me make sense of my feelings.

Why had Theo, who'd looked prettier than ever this morning, seemed to change her mind about me so quickly? Did she just feel sorry for me? Or was Ami right—could it be a trick?

I entered the closest girls' room to find it way more run-down than I'd expected. It had two broken lights overhead and smelled like dampness and fruity body spray. The windows barely let in any light, as they were coated in grime. Instead of warm natural light, the kind Mama spoke love letters about, the bathroom had an unflattering fluorescent-blue sheen.

Deep breaths, I told myself, turning on the closest sink's faucets.

"Deep breaths," I repeated aloud. I felt hot—I unclasped my locket and slipped it into my pocket. Then, to try and center myself, I rinsed my face and neck with cool water and tried to focus on my breathing. "In for four, hold for four—"

"Are you talking to yourself, new girl?"

I froze. With the creaking of the door, three girls came in—and Theo was one of them. Her friends looked just as perfect as her. The girl closest to me, tall and paper pale and slender like a movie star, looked at me like she wanted to spit in my face. And the other, a shorter brown-skinned girl with tortoiseshell glasses and a high ponytail, smiled at me almost shyly.

Nicole and Lily. They shared homeroom with us, and I had a couple other classes with one or both of them. Theo had been whispering and laughing with Nicole after I mentioned Karen Cooper. Lily seemed mostly harmless, at least—an accessory for Nicole. Or a pet.

"I told y'all she was a weirdo," Nicole said.

She moved past me, but not before knocking into me with her giant backpack. I lurched forward, gripping the sink, and watched them in the mirror. Theo locked eyes with me and I swore I almost saw something like sympathy on her face. But I probably was interpreting something wrong.

Nicole pulled a lip gloss tube from the Betsey Johnson purse hanging at her side. "Didn't you see her completely freak out yesterday?"

"I didn't freak out," I said. I was breaking my top rule for keeping under the radar in a new school—I was engaging instead of just keeping quiet and keeping my head down. And honestly, I called it a freak-out myself; I just didn't need this girl to know that. "I had an anxiety attack and a meltdown. I'm autistic."

"So why'd you freak out?" Nicole asked.

I bit the inside of my cheek to stop myself from saying something rude. "I saw a ghost," I said. They already saw me as a weirdo; no sense lying about what happened. "She grabbed my arm."

"You're lying," Nicole scoffed.

"I'm not a liar," I said. "She touched me."

Theo's friends got some kind of thrill out of my comment, chattering with each other and gesturing a bunch, but not Theo. Not Theo, standing near me, still watching me through the mirror. Now I understood what her present had meant even less. I tried to smile at her, to show her it was okay to stand up for me, but my mouth wouldn't move the way I wanted it to. She looked away and adjusted her backpack strap before addressing her friends.

"We gotta go," she said. "We don't wanna be late."

They tucked their makeup back into their bags and moved toward the door as a unit. My grip on the sink loosened as I heard the door creak open again.

"Have fun with the ghosts, new girl! The bathroom's haunted, too!" Nicole sang just before the door swung closed again.

The hum of the light tubes above filled the silence for a few beats.

I sighed and splashed my face lightly, then looked into the mirror again. My eyes looked tired and my shoulders scrunched close to my ears. I was still so tense. An echoed sigh made me freeze up.

No one had come in, and I knew the stalls were empty—

Or, I *thought* the stalls were empty. I didn't dare turn around to check; instead, I shifted my gaze in the mirror. Just in time to catch sight of a pair of shoes slowly stretch toward the floor.

CHAPTER 17

Panic kept me frozen in place. The stall door lazily slid open, and as I turned, I found myself face-to-face with Mac. I sighed in relief, putting a hand against my chest.

"You scared the crap outta me!" My terror became her amusement, making her laugh as she pulled herself up onto a sink to sit.

"Relax," she said while starting to swing her legs. "I didn't want to come out while those other girls were in here."

I nodded, though I was only barely listening. My brain felt like it was vibrating, like there was some frequency pulsing through the bathroom that only I could feel. It made me want to throw up.

"I heard you say you saw a ghost," Mac continued. "Were you scared?"

"Did I hurt your feelings?" I asked instead of answering.

"Eh." She waved a hand, like swatting away my question. "We're good. What was it like?"

Instead of giving a verbal answer, I rolled up my sleeve to show off my burn mark.

Only, it wasn't there anymore.

I rubbed my arm a few times, twisted and turned it around, but there was no trace of the mark anywhere.

"Eva?"

Answering Mac would have been polite, but the surprise of my mark being gone made it impossible to think about social graces. Instead, my head filled only with questions. When did it heal? Why didn't I notice? Had I made the whole thing up?

"I gotta go," I mumbled. I was frustrated at myself—I was probably sabotaging my chances of being friends with Mac, but I couldn't help it. I grabbed my backpack to head for homeroom and kick off my investigation. If I wanted to know what was going on, I needed to be at the source. But the door wouldn't budge. I pulled, and pulled, and pulled and pulled and pulled, but it refused to open. My palms stung as I banged against the door.

"Hey!" I shouted. "Hey, let me out!"

Giggles floated through the door, and soft voices that I couldn't make out. The lights overhead flickered. How could Theo be nice to me fifteen minutes ago but allow her friends to trap me right now?

"Theo, open the door!" I couldn't form the words to yell at

Nicole and Lily, too. I could hear Theo on the other side saying something, but it sounded so far away. Underwater, almost.

The way I'd heard things in the classroom yesterday.

"Mac—!" I turned to Mac, but I found myself alone. Was she hiding in a stall?

Before I could call out to her again, the lights above cracked and blew. Instinctively, I squatted down and covered my head.

"Stop it!" I squeezed my eyes shut.

"Evaaaaaaa . . ."

The whisper returned and I rushed to stand back up. In the dark, through the blackness, I could just make out a tall shape coming closer. It was way too tall to be Mac. I felt like it was watching me. Gliding over the floor ever closer. Glowing lightly, like it had its own light source.

My hands pounded against the door frantically as I yelled for Theo to help me, but I couldn't even hear myself. All I heard was the whispering, the wailing, getting louder and louder. Until I heard nothing at all.

CHAPTER 18

This was all wrong.

As soon as the lights came back on, I knew things were wrong. This wasn't the bathroom I'd walked into—*this* bathroom was clean and warm and inviting. The windows looked worn, but not so stained and grimy. Through the glass, I could easily see a storm surging outside, bending trees and blowing rain sideways. The stalls had only a few permanent marker scribbles on them, and they were painted a tacky pale green instead of black. A row of individual mirrors above each sink replaced the single giant mirror I had been looking into.

"What . . . ?"

None of this made sense. I knew about quick set changes thanks to a brief obsession with theater. But nobody could possibly have turned the old bathroom into this in less than five seconds. I took a few uncertain steps, like the ground might give way if I didn't tread lightly. But the floor was solid, and so was the sink, and the faucet, and the water rushing out after I turned it on. All of it existed, and all of it was a mystery to me.

I'd never gotten zapped into another world before. Another place? Another time? Not knowing where or when or *how* I was wherever I was scared me to death. But there was no time to let anxiety take over.

Conversation outside came closer. I ducked into a stall. Peeking through the crack, I could see a small group of girls in uniforms, gathered at the sinks, talking about an upcoming dance. Their hairstyles looked like the kind I saw while thumbing through MawMaw Septine's old photo albums.

They didn't notice me. When they left, I waited a moment before following. But as soon as I stepped out of the bathroom, I stopped in my tracks.

The hallway couldn't have been more different. The lockers stood on the wrong side of the hall, classrooms that should have been there weren't, a banner about the fiftieth anniversary celebration stretched across one wall, none of Miss Noon's decorations were on what should have been my homeroom door—

My homeroom door. The door to the haunted classroom.

If I were in a cartoon, I'd make a really loud, nervous gulp. But my mouth felt too dry to work anything up. I thought about running back to the bathroom, trying to figure out how to get back to familiarity. But MawMaw Septine would say I was being shown this for a reason, and I had to admit, I wanted to figure that reason out. And besides, if I was gonna figure out the haunting, I had to try squashing my nerves.

With so many other students wandering the halls, I figured no one would notice me slipping into that classroom. Giant chalkboard, desks arranged in a circle, ancient crusty maps hung so that they could be pulled down like cheap window shades . . . This was it. The center of the tragedy.

Suddenly, I couldn't breathe. *I shouldn't be here* ran circles around my head over and over. My hand scrambled for the comfort of my opal locket to ground myself. Or maybe wake myself up. Maybe I got so scared by the tall shadow spirit that I just . . . passed out? I knew I'd taken it off and put it in a pocket, so why couldn't I feel it?

But it all felt way too real. So many heavy, loud sensations sent my head spinning. I could smell lunch being prepared somewhere close by, something heavy on garlic. Students skirted around me and the unpleasant fabric of their uniforms scratched against my skin.

Sensory overload gripped my body to the point that I thought I felt the floor shaking.

No.

Actually.

The floor *really* shook.

A slow-dance-like tremble came to life with a groan. I

steadied myself using a desk as the hallway chatter grew louder. They must have felt it, too. But soon the floor steadied, like an earthquake had passed.

"Excuse me? Are you meant to be here?"

I gasped and whipped around. The face staring back at me nearly made me fall over.

Nothing was dripping or hanging or oozing from her this time, but her face was unmistakable. The ghastly woman. The mournful ghost hiding among the trees. Alive, in the flesh, speaking to me, skin pale but free of dampness. Her face twisted in concern and her hands came together in front of her as she leaned toward me.

"Are you all right?" the ghastly woman asked. "Where are you supposed to be right now?"

Her voice sounded like a soft chime, a hug from a beloved relative. She was comfort in a way I usually only felt from my immediate family. I instantly wanted to move forward and put my arms around her and tell her all my problems. But I couldn't tell her anything; I couldn't even open my mouth to try and explain why I was there.

"The bell is about to ring," she said, trying again to get me to speak. "If you tell me what class—"

"Mrs. Perrin?" The tall woman and I both shifted focus to the student interrupting us. I gasped. Another familiar face.

I was looking right at Mac.

CHAPTER 19

There was no mistaking her—she smiled brightly at the ghastly woman, Mrs. Perrin, her tooth gap front and center. She was dressed in a uniform but had the same beat-up Chuck Taylors, same frizzy hair, same pudgy cheeks. She tilted her head a little.

"Could I maybe stay in your classroom for my free period?" Mac—or someone who looked way, *way* too much like Mac—asked.

My stomach dropped when maybe-Mac looked right at me. I took a step back as if that might help her not see me. The way she stared made me shiver.

Mrs. Perrin walked closer to put a hand on Mac's shoulder. "Give me a moment, Sutton," she said.

Sutton? The name pinged something in my memory; I hadn't heard it often since we grandkids weren't allowed to call adults by their first names, but Nanay, my dad's mom, was a Sutton. What were the odds that my grandma and the ghost haunting me shared the same name?

A bell rang and students flooded into the classroom. Mrs. Perrin turned back to me with a look that seemed like she wanted to apologize. With the excited chatter in the room, I couldn't hear what she was saying to Mac—Sutton—but it made the girl nod and walk up an aisle of desks. Her eyes fixed on me again, her expression an unreadable blankness. A second bell rang, and she took a seat near the back of the room.

Mrs. Perrin turned back to me. "Are you new? Did the office send you here?"

I wasn't sure what to say, so I just nodded, and she pointed me to a seat.

Mrs. Perrin began writing on the chalkboard behind her desk. A date, one that made no sense for me to be around for. Almost exactly fifty years ago.

"So today, my darlings," she said with a smile that held a surprise, "we're going to do something a little different. In honor of the upcoming anniversary celebration, we'll be discussing the history of our lovely school! Isn't that fun?"

Grumbles and rumblings reminded me of how unenthusiastic students around the world could be whenever teachers tried to force excitement. And apparently students throughout time, too. But Mrs. Perrin seemed unbothered, and her smile never once fell. Instead, she looked at me and motioned again for me to take a seat. The only spot left for me was right beside Mac. Sutton. Whichever.

I tried not to stare or shake. I didn't have my opal to offer some comfort. But Mrs. Perrin's history lesson distracted me enough to forget about being scared of Sutton.

The way she told the story of the school brought the whole founding to life. She danced around the front of the classroom, making large gestures and drawing in the attention of the whole class. If I lived now—well, then-now—I just knew I would've adored being in her class. I got so wrapped up in watching her, listening to her talk about the Friends of Lafayette Falls Lake, the way they found this empty, unclaimed land, the opening of the school almost fifty years ago, that I almost missed the shift in the room that radiated from Sutton.

When I looked over at her, her hands were clenched into fists on top of the desk. Her face clenched, too, and her leg bounced fast enough to vibrate the desk of the person in front of her. The air chilled fast, my breath puffing out in front of me. But only me. Just as Mrs. Perrin began reading from the school's original mission statement written by the Friends, thunder boomed. The lights above popped and left the whole room in darkness. Some students screamed in surprise, and Mrs. Perrin tried to reassure them that we were safe.

"You're lying," Sutton announced, rage in her eyes.

Mrs. Perrin lost her sunny smile for a second. It came back covered by a few clouds. "Sutton, why would you say that? Of course I'm not lying."

Sutton glowered at her and stood, suddenly backlit by a flash of lightning outside. "One way or another, the truth always comes out."

She walked toward the door, calm as can be. Her footsteps pounded on the floor, echoing almost as loudly as the thunder rumbling closer and closer. She stopped at the door, then turned. Her eyes scanned the room until she found her target—me.

She smiled at me just as more lightning struck. Something deep in my core felt shaken. It wasn't a friendly smile; I knew easily how to recognize those. This smile seemed strange. Secretive.

Evil.

I watched her mouth move, but lipreading was never my strong suit. And then she was gone, slipping out the door and slamming it behind herself. Not even two seconds later, I felt the ground vibrate again. The movement swelled to a steady, forceful shake. Groaning and creaking drowned out confused yells and screaming thunder. Mrs. Perrin tried once more to calm her students, but control of the class was long since lost. And when an earsplitting crack came, more frenzy did, too.

I ran for the door. The knob refused to turn, no matter how hard I tried. Another crack of noise hurt my ears, and this time, a beam from the ceiling crashed down. A girl nearby, one of the ones I'd seen in the bathroom, shrieked. The beam had struck her and trapped her, and her legs were bent in a way legs shouldn't. I had to look away for the sake of my stomach.

More parts of the ceiling tumbled down. A shock of frigid rain poured in. Lightning struck so close that the hairs on my arms stood straight out. The air was literally electrified. Burning wood, probably whatever tree had been struck outside, made the whole room smell like a campfire.

The ground shook harder. I slammed my shoulder into the door, again and again and again. Other students pounded and banged and kicked the door along with me. But it wouldn't budge. I peered out the slender glass rectangle set in the door. Maybe someone was passing in the hallway; they could open the door and let us out.

There, on the other side of the glass, Sutton looked back at me. That cold smile made me shudder. I almost tripped backing away.

Right by my feet, a crack started to form. I scrambled out of the way as it widened. With a horrifying cracking noise, the whole floor split apart, violent and jagged. Desks and students toppled over, the half of the room that I stood in began to sink lower, and lower, and lower. I had to crane my neck up to see the other half.

Mrs. Perrin lay on the ground at the edge, hand outstretched toward me, toward anyone who could reach her; her fingertips grazed mine for half a second, but I couldn't keep my grip. Some other students jumped to try and catch hold, but mud and dirt and grime sloughed off the split area and kept us all down. And still, the earth shook.

CHAPTER 20

I couldn't breathe.

Here I was, stuck in a pit, still falling

falling

falling

with people I didn't know, in a place I shouldn't be. I tried desperately to climb up, to use some tricks Egypt taught me about climbing trees, but my shoes just kept slipping. A rock tumbled over the side, missing me by inches. It startled me so much that I flailed back onto my butt. And right then, one of the light fixtures crashed down next to me.

I rolled out of the way just barely in time. More slippery mud fell as the crack grew, and I could see bits of something in the sludge. Something grimy and near-white, long, thin, like bones. Another ceiling piece snapped loose and smashed into the pit. Mud and white shards flew from the impact. A skull knocked free and rolled right toward my feet.

Not *like* bones. *Definitely* bones.

My screaming seemed to echo as I curled up to try and protect my head. Around me, more of the ceiling slammed into the floor, into this pit, scarily close to hitting me. So many things fell, so much mud, so many bones. Something brushed my hand and I jumped with another loud scream.

"Eva!"

The underwater sound again. My heart probably wouldn't be able to take beating any faster. I just knew I was going to die in this pit. Whoever yelled my name kept saying it, kept sounding muffled and dreamy. The rain, the students screaming, the thunder—it all floated away. Whispers replaced them. Whispers right in my head. *Eva . . . home . . . family . . . Eva . . . home . . .*

"Eva! Eva, can you hear me?"

When the whispering subsided, I could finally tell who was calling me. Not a ghost, or some skeleton, or Sutton-Mac. Miss Noon. I relaxed, just barely, and shifted to look up.

There was no mud surrounding me. There was no pit. There weren't any bones. Only Miss Noon, looking down at me, concern and confusion furrowing her brows.

She drew her hand back. "Eva, what happened?" she asked softly.

I pushed myself into sitting up.

I was back in the girls' bathroom, and it looked fine. No cracks in the floor, no ceiling collapse, no screaming students falling into the earth. All I could see were the faces of some of my classmates crowded around the doorway—Theo included—staring at me like I'd just detached my own head.

Nothing made sense.

The words I needed to use to answer Miss Noon clumped together at the back of my throat and refused to go any further. Even taking some deep breaths to try and calm myself failed to get them to move. I started instead to sign to her.

I can't speak.

Miss Noon tilted her head to one side and furrowed her mouth, like she didn't have the words, either. I knew her signing skills were limited to a few basics Daddy had taught her to help with me, but I couldn't remember exactly what she knew. Evidently, it didn't include what I'd just said.

"She said she can't talk right now." Theo, clear as crystal, spoke up. We locked eyes for a second before I had to look away.

"Thank you, Theo," Miss Noon said. She sighed and held her hands out to me. "C'mon, sweetheart," she said, and her voice felt like a warm blanket.

It lasted only a second before a shiver ran through me. I reached out to Miss Noon and immediately froze just before taking her hands. All over my fingers, stuck beneath my nails—was mud.

CHAPTER 21

My hands still didn't feel clean, even after washing them a fourth time. I stopped myself from getting up yet again; Nurse Bobbi already looked way too concerned about me. Instead, I rubbed my fingertips against the soft fabric of the inside of my hoodie pouch pocket.

None of it was real. I wasn't in the past. I didn't fall into a sinkhole. I hadn't come face-to-face with the ghastly woman. Miss Noon had told the nurse that I'd passed out in the bathroom and needed to rest a bit. I'd been set up with some apple juice and a turkey sandwich to try and raise my blood sugar.

But I felt fine. I'd never passed out without being sick before. I had mud on my hands, for crying out loud. Fainting never spontaneously tossed dirt on anyone in the history of medical emergencies. My brain felt fuzzy, though—too overloaded to argue with either grown-up. So I lay on the cot and sipped my juice and nibbled my sandwich. I counted the ceiling tiles. I ran through Karen Cooper's first EP in my head. I slipped my locket back on and clamped the chain between my teeth. Anything to avoid hyperfixating on what had just happened to me.

"You saw the accident, huh?"

My whole body tensed. I didn't want to see Mac, so of course she found me here in the nurse's office. I would have felt differently if I hadn't run into her in my vision.

Dream?

Hallucination?

Whatever it was, Mac was there, being called a whole different name, looking at me like we shared a secret that only *she* knew. And now Mac was here beside my cot, sporting a similar but friendlier teasing smile. Whatever this was, whatever was happening with her, I *needed* to get to the bottom of it.

Her question felt like a threat, but I couldn't understand why.

My hands shook, my fingers squeezing tighter around my bottle of juice. I couldn't relax around her. Even the gentle sound of the class dismissal bell made me jump. Being near Mac after what happened felt . . . wrong. I couldn't get that smile out of my head . . . that evil look in her eye.

She didn't seem to care. "How do you feel now?" she asked. "Weird? Do you think you saw what happened for a reason?"

"A reason like what?" I asked. Mac shrugged. "Mac. Do you know something? This is important. Please don't be coy."

She dodged my question. "You and me, peas in a pod. A spooky pod. We gotta look out for each other in that case. Maybe we should do some digging together."

The nurse's office grew quiet. I knew Mac was waiting for me to say something. But my brain felt like scrambled eggs and my lips refused to move. Another bell chimed to signal the start of the next class period. But Mac didn't leave. Nurse Bobbi walked right past the door without asking her where she was supposed to be.

"I like your necklace," Mac said. It was nearly a song, the way she spoke. That secret-keeping smile crept back. I slid away from her as subtly as I could. Once I felt a safe distance from her, I looked down to confirm what I already knew. My necklace lay against my chest, inside my hoodie and my shirt, the gold pendant cool against my skin. So how could she . . . "Can I see it?"

"Mac . . ."

I looked up to interrogate her. Except, she wasn't there.

She wasn't anywhere.

A chill tiptoed along my spine as I whipped around to see if she had moved to the other side of me. But she hadn't. I was alone. And I suddenly didn't want to be.

I scooped up my things and hustled to the door. I'd be a little late for my next class, but at least I'd be surrounded and safe. Maybe.

CHAPTER 22

In class, the other students whispered about me, at least it seemed like they were—they'd take peeks at me and cup their mouths and snicker with their friends. A couple of times the teacher approached me to ask in that soft, pitying voice if I was doing okay. I don't even remember answering. And as soon as class was dismissed, I hurried out into the hall. Miss Noon should've been back in her classroom, and I needed desperately to talk to her.

I made it seventeen steps before the Brats decided to block my way, led by Nicole.

My stomach clenched. They definitely wanted to start something, I could feel it. Theo had an apology in her eyes and for reasons I couldn't figure out, it made me angry. If she wanted, she could've just told her friends to leave me alone. But she didn't.

I backed up a little, hands blindly fumbling to reach the lockers for support.

"Can't believe you freaked out like that in the bathroom," Nicole sneered. She folded her arms over her chest and stared at me. She wanted a response, I realized. She probably wanted me to cry or get upset or something. Instead, I just stared right back.

The silence got to be too much for them. They fidgeted and exchanged looks until finally, Lily spoke up. "How'd you get that mud on you, though?" she asked as she pushed her glasses up with her middle finger.

For a second, I almost thought she meant I was muddy right now. I glanced down, but nothing was there. And I'd washed my hands enough times that they felt raw. "I dunno," I said. "It just . . . happened." When I looked to Theo, she quickly looked away. Was she watching me? "Why do you care?"

"You didn't tell anyone we locked you in, did you?" Nicole asked. I shook my head. "Good. You should keep it that way."

"Or what?" I laughed. Girls like this always had more threats in them than action. I wasn't in the mood to play that game. "Are you gonna beat me up?"

"Maybe." Nicole sniffed. She stepped closer to me, and Lily clasped her wrist.

"What are you doing?" Lily whispered.

"I don't like you," Nicole stated. By now, other kids had started to gather around us, hushed whispers and phones sneakily recording everything.

"I don't care," I said before really thinking about it. Dr. Choudhury talked a lot about not saying things in my head out loud without considering how they might be taken. But I didn't care if I hurt Nicole's feelings.

The growing crowd vibrated with a low hum, like I'd said something really offensive. And maybe I had, judging by Nicole's face pinching up. She stepped forward again and I had to look up a bit—she was at least three inches taller than me. But she was skinnier. I had gotten some tips from PawPaw Thibodeaux about fighting before Mama had put a stop to it. I could at least get a few licks in if I had to.

"Come on, Nicki," Theo said. "Let's just leave her alone."

"You think you're so special," Nicole scoffed. Another step closer to me. I had nowhere to go, since I was already pressed against the lockers. I felt boxed in. "You and your little weirdo freak-outs."

The crowd around us jostled and eventually spit Ami out right in front of me. They raised an eyebrow, like they wanted to know if I needed help. I started to shake my head, but they were already gathering their curls into a ponytail.

"Hey! Leave her alone," Ami called out as they moved forward.

"Oh great, now your little freak friend is here, too," said Nicole.

"Nicole, that's enough," Lily said as Ami moved even closer. Lily pulled at Nicole's arm, but Nicole slipped free. Now I understood how getting Nicole to back off might not have been within Theo's power. Some people were just determined to take down anyone who was different.

Instead of walking away like her friends suggested, she pushed me. My head knocked against the locker, and everyone around us got more riled up. I didn't even think—I just reached out and shoved. Nicole nearly fell over backward, colliding with Lily in a way that looked painful. I almost apologized. But before I could, she shoved me again.

I hated fighting. Watching fights stressed me out, and now *being* in one felt even worse. Nicole pulled at my hair, my clothes, tried to yank me down to the ground. All I could do was try to defend and block. Ami snatched Lily's ponytail to try and keep her off me. Theo shouted for Nicole to back off, some kids shouted for me to punch Nicole, others started chanting "*FIGHT! FIGHT!*" Everything overwhelmed me and I wanted to run, but Nicole wouldn't let me go. A sudden scream cut through the noise and silenced everyone.

It was Nicole. As soon as she screamed, she let go of me, backing away just as a few teachers approached us.

"She bit me!" Nicole was shrieking. "That weirdo bit me!"

CHAPTER 23

Two little trickles of blood slid down Nicole's arm and over her fingers, which were squeezing her forearm tight. All eyes turned to me. They watched me like I was some kind of monster, like I'd ripped her face off and eaten it in front of everyone. But I hadn't done anything except try to keep her off me. I hadn't bit anyone since I was a toddler; the taste of skin bugged me too much for that.

My mind spun at double speed as the biology teacher ushered Ami, Theo, Nicole, Lily, and me to Miss Alice's office. Nicole kept yelling, the other two talking at the same time, but I didn't understand any of them. Whooshing in my ears muffled everything, the quiet thump of my heartbeat the only sound sitting just beneath. My stomach threatened to empty itself out. I was going to be in big trouble. This was one step closer to strike three. I would be out, and my parents would be disappointed, and I'd wind up a middle school dropout busking for change and living in a converted school bus with a shaggy dog named Scooter.

Which, if I thought about it, sounded kind of fun, but still. I couldn't handle the idea of being in trouble.

Hot tears fell. I was doomed.

The others sat as far from me and Ami as they could, and I tried to sniffle quietly so they would forget I was even there. Every now and then, they'd look over at me—Nicole with anger, Lily with maybe sympathy, and Theo . . . I couldn't figure out Theo's face. Which gave me a totally-not-weird reason to keep looking at her. It was research, I told myself. I had to build up my library of expressions to understand for any future conversations. Dr. Choudhury would be proud.

Well. As long as I didn't tell her about the fight.

At least, I told myself, Ami still had my back. They held my hand and let me sit in silence, but I knew if I wanted to talk, they'd listen. That was something I never had in other schools.

". . . can't even believe she bit me." Nicole's voice cut through the noise in my head. I watched her uncover her arm to show off her wound to the others. And I watched her swipe some blood away.

Beneath the blood, the bite mark stood out against Nicole's skin. Red and swollen and angry. It looked like it hurt a lot.

I squinted and leaned forward to see her arm better. The bite mark wasn't very big, so it couldn't have been an adult. And it was definitely human. But there on the top row, clear as crystal, was a gap in the front teeth.

A gap.

Mac.

That couldn't be right. If Mac had gotten in between us, I would have seen her. I would have spoken to her. But the bite had a gap just like Mac's.

How?

As soon as I saw that mark, the coldness I'd felt before came back. Something in the doorway pulled my focus, and when I looked over, Mac was peeking around the doorframe at me. She smiled, small and shy, then motioned for me to come closer.

I shook my head, but she waved her hand more aggressively. No one else seemed to notice her. I shot a glance at Miss Alice's closed door, murmured to Ami that I'd be right back, and went to stand just out of sight in the hallway with Mac.

She was the last person I wanted to be close to. "What do you want?"

Instead of answering, she pointed toward Nicole, then gave a thumbs-up.

"Did you bite her?" I asked in a hushed voice. "Why would you do that? And *how?*"

"She was bothering you," Mac whispered back. "I told you. We're peas in a pod. I'm protecting you."

"I don't want that," I hissed. "That was messed up, and now *I'm* gonna get in trouble. You can't just bite people, Mac."

"Who's Mac?" I jumped at Ami's sudden appearance. They stood just behind me and observed me with confusion. I started to explain what happened, but Mac wasn't there.

And I didn't know if Mac was *ever* there.

Much as it scared me, I needed to know exactly why. My future at Blythe depended on it.

CHAPTER 24

Daddy had to be tired of me by this point.

I'd sat outside the headmaster's office for what felt like forever, waiting to be called in and told I was expelled. But Theo, Nicole, and Lily went into the office first, and when they left Ami and I were told we were free to go. I spent the whole rest of the day with my mind swimming with questions, but I should have known this would catch up with me. I should have known the school would call Daddy.

He didn't *look* tired of me as he sat on the other side of the video call, and he didn't say it, but anxiety in my head screamed it at me. I knew he should've been busy with cleaning up MawMaw Septine's home; yet here he was looking at me with concern painting his face. I started to idly look up how to put yourself up for adoption. He deserved better than having to deal with me.

I wanted to tuck myself away into the closet like I might've done in any other non-haunted place, even though I knew Vee wouldn't be in until hours from now because of drama club. I often felt safer in tighter spaces when the big wide world got to be too much. But the closet scared the life outta me, and I certainly wasn't about to put myself in harm's way. So I sat on my bed instead, pressed against the wall, hoping really hard that I wasn't in mega trouble. A lecture was coming, I could feel it. Maybe if I didn't look his way, he'd let it go.

"So." Daddy tapped his purple nails against a water bottle in front of him. We'd gotten matching manicures in my favorite color just before he brought me to Blythe. "Miss Noon rang me. Can we talk about why you got sent out of class and then to the headmaster's office today? Again?"

"I just had a really bad panic attack," I said. Which was true. But I didn't want to explain any deeper than that. Not to Daddy. "And this girl, she pushed me, and you're always saying don't start nothing but don't hesitate to finish it and I didn't bite her, I *swear*, it—"

"Eva, if you're having a hard time—"

"I'm not," I insisted. My breath started to catch in my chest.

Daddy sighed and leaned back against the worn-out recliner he sat in. That used to be PawPaw Thibodeaux's seat. It would probably go to a donation center when everything was said and done. Or the curb. Or the dump. The thought of all our memories woven into the scratchy burnt-orange fabric of that chair being tossed into the trash made my eyes sting with tears I wasn't ready to cry.

"I can't come to your rescue every time," Daddy said. "I love you and I'll protect you no matter the circumstances. For the rest of my life. But I want you to try and figure out a way to protect *yourself*, too. Do you think you can handle that? Like, for real? Because you keep saying yes and then you keep having trouble."

"I'm sorry," I said. Crying made me feel like a baby, but tears made their way down my cheeks against everything I wanted. I sniffled and rubbed my face, hoping being rough would somehow make my body stop this "feelings" nonsense. "I'm sorry, please don't send me away."

"Eva . . . No one's gonna send you away," Daddy said. "You think I'd do that? C'mon now."

"You and Mama think I'm a burden." I cried harder. This was not the behavior of a seventh grader. Everything about this was embarrassing and yet I couldn't stop. "You're gonna send me somewhere for difficult children and you're gonna get divorced because you fight about me all the time and Egypt will hate me because now we have a broken home and I'll never have a family again!"

My eyes blurred from tears. Between the ghosts and the threat of rejection, I couldn't take anymore. Every sadness I'd felt for months, maybe years, welled up and crashed out of me. A real, proper, disgusting snotty cry. Definitely a middle school low point.

"Hey. Doods. Can you pick the phone back up, please?"

It took some moments before I could. Daddy shook on the screen no matter how much I tried to keep my hand steady. Eventually, I gave up. I put the phone on my pillow, pulling the kickstand out to steady it. Then I lay down so I could actually see him.

"I promise it's just your imagination running away with you," he said. Well, more like sang. I usually laughed at him slipping song lyrics into conversation, but I didn't feel up to it this time. "We disagree sometimes about a lot of things. Not just you, and never to the point that we might get divorced. And Egypt adores you. She could never disown you. And we would *never* think you're a burden. I just want you to feel comfortable and happy at Blythe. And in general. That's all."

"Okay." My voice barely escaped me. "I really did see a ghost, though."

"Eva Amari . . ." Daddy sighed. "Tell you what. If you see a ghost again, get a picture."

"Ghosts don't show up on camera," I mumbled.

"They might if you ask nicely." He grinned way too widely for what wasn't actually a very funny joke. And he stayed like that, the way he would when he insisted on getting one of us to break and smile at him. "Eh? Ehhhh?"

"You're not funny," I said while trying to hide my smile behind my arm. "MawMaw Septine woulda believed me."

Almost as soon as I said it, I felt awful for it. He stopped smiling; his shoulders fell. He nodded, just barely, then sat up to be closer to the camera.

"I believe that *you* believe," he said. "And I know it's been hard lately. I apologize for making you feel like you're not being heard. I hear you. Whatcha think MawMaw would tell you to do?"

My grandmother, fierce and wild and unafraid, would've said I needed to toughen up. To let the haints know I'm not scared because I've got light in me. That they can't hurt me unless I let them. Because I've got some pretty resilient blood running through me, and even at my most scared, I'm still a warrior. No matter what.

I knew what needed to be done. I needed to step up and act like I know who I am. Even if maybe I wasn't entirely sure. I could be brave and not let the ghosts of Blythe Academy run me. Not when I risked losing my first real friends and having to start over at yet another new school. No hecking way. It was time for me to dry my tears and figure this all out so I could get free of this fear.

No. Matter. What.

CHAPTER 25

When dinnertime rolled around, I finally shuffled my way out of my room, smacking right into Theo.

We both bounced back, and her cheeks got a little darker. "Sorry," she said. Definitely not the way she reacted when we ran into each other the first time. "Um. Sorry if this is weird. I guess I just kinda showed up—"

"What do you want?" I asked.

Her eyes widened. "I just wanted to say sorry," she said. "Nicki is . . . Well. We *all* are kind of mean, I guess. Which I know is . . . pretty crappy. I guess I didn't think too much about it until . . . And I tried to tell her that you're . . . I mean . . ."

She shifted her weight from foot to foot, holding her arm and rubbing it. She was nervous. I understood nervous. But I didn't know how to help her be less nervous in that moment. So I just waited for her to finish her thought.

After a few more starts that went nowhere, she sighed. "My brother is autistic," she said. This time, it was my eyes that widened. "And I guess I felt bad you . . . I mean, I kinda guessed before you said . . . Not to say everybody with autism is the same, but . . . I'm sorry, is all. You didn't deserve any of that. Maybe we can be friends? I can try harder to make Nicki and everybody else leave you alone."

"Why?" I asked. It made no sense to me. Just because a family member had the same medical diagnosis as me, she needed to be nice to me now? If people just started out being nice, this would be so much less confusing.

"Well, because you don't deserve to be picked on," Theo said. "I was a jerk. And I'm sorry. Can you just say you forgive me, please?"

My reaction whenever someone apologized was to forgive them. It was part of the social norms, after all. Even if they didn't mean it. Even if I didn't feel it. But I still had my grandmother in mind, and that pushed me to be a little less accepting of an empty apology. I felt relieved that she didn't seem to hate me anymore, but I deserved friends who treated me right all the time, not just in private.

"No," I said as I shook my head. Her face fell. "You have to put actions to words. If you felt sorry before, why didn't you stop the fight? So it's not real. You don't get to feel guilty about being a jerk just because I have a disability. *Nobody* deserves to be picked on. Maybe I can forgive you if you act better."

I wrapped up my comment with a nod. Something like pride started to mix into my anxiety; I tried to remember everything my parents taught me about forgiveness and honesty and sincerity and not letting people walk all over me.

I held my head high for the first time since getting to this school and started toward the dining hall. I defended myself and I spoke up for myself. Good for me.

"Good for you." I froze. That was Mac's voice, and she sounded way too close for comfort. If I turned, she'd be right there. I knew it.

And I knew turning was a bad idea, but . . .

Ash caked Mac's hair. Her beautiful brown skin was now charred and splotchy and split open like a cracked porcelain doll. Embers jumped from all around her and fluttered to the ground. I gasped and nearly gagged—I could almost *taste* burning flesh. Clouded eyes, a soot-stained singed white dress, a giant creepy grin—and that tooth gap.

"Stay with me, Eva," she rasped.

I never ran so fast in my life.

CHAPTER 26

After my heart stopped racing and Vee and Ami cheered me up over dinner, I felt good for a few days. The school ghosts must have pitied me; nothing happened at all right up to the weekend. I slept well, I managed to eat, Nicole steered clear of me, I didn't see Miss Alice at all. And I kind of had . . . friends?

Maybe not *friends* quite yet, but definitely friendly. I ate lunch every day with Ami, Vee, and a few of their friends. I told them all I could about Karen Cooper and gardening and art. And they taught me about K-pop and fishkeeping and mountain biking. I wished I'd been able to make friends sooner at other schools; it felt kind of amazing to have people interested in and engaged with me.

They absorbed me into their bubble, without expectations or judgment or the threat of it all being an overly complicated plan to embarrass me somehow. They were nice. Like real nice, and it took me a few days to accept that they meant it. Instead of laughing *at* me, they laughed *with* me. I even got to lie around with my head on Vee's knee—for a few minutes. I didn't want to push my luck.

By Saturday, I'd all but forgotten about being so scared. I just felt normal. For once.

Miss Noon and Miss Eugenie, a wisp of a woman who always looked like she'd received tragic news about the Civil War via the pony express, took a group of us from the dorms into town. Some people needed to shop for toiletries and snacks for their rooms, though I had a fresh stock of everything I needed since I'd just moved in. But Vee insisted I come and see the town's oldest business, a general store called Haley's Feed Company. Nothing about that sounded interesting to me, but she was excited and I owed it to her after talking for two hours straight about poisonous plants of the Ozarks. So I quietly followed her lead and marveled at a general store still being in operation in the twenty-first century.

Immediately, the smell of apple cinnamon assaulted my nostrils. The store had way too many air fresheners, to the point where I almost felt nauseous. Vee spoke at hyperspeed as she led me around Haley's—which, I noticed, had way more than just food for livestock. Between the smell and the noise, I felt uncomfortably overstimulated. I excused myself from Vee's personal tour and tried to find a spot in the store that wasn't too noisy or stinky.

I slipped behind a dusty beaded curtain into a tiny museum-type room. Artifacts were all over, antique memories important to the store, the town, the nation. Little American flags, presidential portraits, Norman Rockwell paintings. Mama had taught me that tchotchkes like these were called Americana, and part of me expected to see something vaguely—or maybe not-so-vaguely—racist any second, like I had with Mama. But so far, so nontraumatic.

The smell of mildew filled the room. Like something had gotten wet at some point and not dried all the way. Still unpleasant, but easier to deal with than overly sweet apples. Ads for products from the fifties and even earlier dotted the walls, an old military gun from the Revolutionary War rested in a glass case, and a different case holding a mangled pair of pants stood in one corner right next to a massive taxidermy bear. The bear—Big Dan, according to the plaque nearby—apparently stalked around Riker's Bend for weeks scaring the bejeebus outta the townsfolk. At some point, it attacked the original owner of the store, Patrick Haley. Haley survived, although his pants got pretty messed up. He shot the poor bear and had him stuffed.

I hated Haley, I decided right then and there.

"Sorry, Dan," I said, mumbling so I was less likely to be overheard talking to a dead bear. I reached out and patted his paw as a comfort. Layers of dust poofed up, and I sneezed as my hand kicked up a cloud of allergens.

"Gesundheit."

Theo slipped into the room and stepped closer, standing beside me near a wall of newspaper clippings with bins of vintage candy beneath. We locked eyes, but I looked away pretty fast. Eye contact made my stomach feel weird, anyway, but looking at Theo was especially challenging. She made me feel too much of everything all at the same time. I was proud that I had stood up for myself, but I was also kind of kicking myself for saying we couldn't be friends. But at least I caught a second of her smile—her lips tinted violet this time, with flecks of gold glitter that shined beneath the warm lights above us.

"Thanks," I said. She reached out and grabbed a small baggie, then handed one to me, too. "Oh, um. I'm only supposed to use my money for—"

"My treat," Theo said. Before I could protest again, she dropped a couple of white-wrapped tubes into my baggie. "These are super good. You won't regret it."

"Are you trying to feel less guilty about being mean to me?" I asked.

There was a pause, and then: "A little bit."

124

"Don't."

"Okay."

We picked out candy in silence, although my bag ended up pretty empty aside from some things Theo insisted I try. Too many unknowns felt overwhelming, so I just let her choose for me. I held my bag out to her, and she met my hand to take it. The second her fingers slid against mine, I thought I might throw up from nerves. *Illogical*, I told myself in my head. I squeezed my locket tight enough that the hinge left marks in my palm. Theo was just a girl. A *really* pretty girl. Nothing to get so flustered over.

As she continued looking for the perfect candy, I stared at some of the wall hangings more closely. A collage of news clippings caught my eye. They were nearly buried behind a display of dented, rusty soup cans, but I could see just faintly a mention of a storm. Curiosity pulled me away from Theo; maybe it was the storm that collapsed the school. That certainly seemed noteworthy enough to put on a wall.

Sure as sherbet, the article talked about the fiftieth anniversary and the storm that ruined the whole thing. I squinted and stepped closer—and gasped.

Mrs. Perrin's face grinned from inside the frame. The headline above her picture chilled me—TEACHER, STUDENTS PERISH IN FREAK STORM. Some of the article was hard to read from my angle, but it told the story of the storm and the classroom collapse almost exactly like I experienced it.

Mrs. Perrin's wasn't the only photograph printed. Smaller portraits of the kids who died in the storm ran along with the article. Row after row of school portraits, names in tiny print underneath. And there, in the fourth row, dead center, was Mac—Sutton, according to my vision—and her sinister smile.

Chills overpowered the butterflies I felt from being near Theo. None of this made sense. Mac, in my vision, had been in the classroom that day going by Sutton. She'd watched me struggle to escape. Did she lock us in on purpose? And the last time I saw Mac she appeared burned, but . . . the accident had nothing to do with fire. What—

"Oh wow." Theo bumped my shoulder and knocked me out of my spiral of questions. "That girl looks kinda like you."

". . . Which one?"

"That girl," she repeated. She lifted her finger and pointed a glittery pink nail right at Mac. "You kinda look alike, don't you think?"

CHAPTER 27

I didn't think. No part of me ever connected Mac's looks to my own.

Part of it had to do with not having all that strong a mental map of what I looked like. It sounded strange to a lot of people, but I looked at myself even less than I looked at other people. Mama often teased me about my aversion to mirrors, but it never mattered much to me. I liked clothes, but I didn't need a mirror to see what I was putting on. And makeup was kind of cool, but I never bothered wearing it, so I didn't need a mirror for that, either.

But I knew what my grandmother looked like as a child from years of obsessively looking at her old photos. And I knew I looked a lot like her. So looking at Mac with that in mind, I saw it—I saw bits of dad's mom, Nanay, and so I saw bits of me.

Not that I wanted to. But now that Theo had pointed it out, it embedded in my brain. I had to stop looking at it. I had to force my brain not to fixate. Too late, I knew. I had already lost track of how much time had passed when I reached out to try and wipe a bit of dust away and—

"Eva?" Miss Noon stood there with Theo when I whirled around. She raised one eyebrow. "Is everything okay?"

". . . Yes." It took a moment to find my voice.

"Theo was worried; she said you just stopped responding to her."

Concern was all over Theo's face, and I wasn't sure why. I hadn't heard her saying anything. What were they even talking about?

Miss Noon approached and laid the back of her hand on my forehead. "Well, you're not feverish," she said. She glanced at the wall in front of us, then did a cartoon-style double take. Her face contorted into something unreadable—like maybe she'd seen something too weird for words. Her hands gripped my shoulders a little too tightly. "Come on. Let's go join the others."

I didn't want to. I wanted to stay with the article clipping, to try and find more information somewhere on the wall. I felt like I *needed* to stay. But Miss Noon steered me over to where everyone else was waiting. They surrounded a TV playing a local commercial about the anniversary celebration. Admittedly, the whole thing looked fun—carnival rides, all kinds of fair food, live music. A weirdly wholesome event to celebrate a tragedy. And nobody seemed to care.

The commercial turned my stomach; all the smiling, happy people felt disrespectful. And I didn't know why I felt angry about it, as if they were personally hurting me. Sometimes my empathy was out of control; I'd often get so overwhelmed with someone else's emotions that I'd just freeze up. Which I'd learned was pretty common for autistic people—on the outside, it seemed like not caring at all, when really the problem was caring too much.

"Eva!"

I yelped and turned around swinging. Ami laughed as they dodged. "Whoa okay, sorry!"

"Don't *do* that!" I snapped. All the amusement drained out of their face. "What is *wrong* with you?!"

"Eva—"

"She doesn't like being scared like that!" My voice was too loud. Other kids, other townsfolk browsing around, started to stare. The anger that rose up in me fell away. I watched Ami's shoulders slump. They frowned.

"Fine," they said. "*She* can sit by herself on the way home."

Before I could try and stop them, Ami walked away. They stood with Vee near the cash registers, and I knew what was going to happen next. I would lose my friends because I'd snapped for no reason. And I'd be an outcast at Blythe forever. I wanted to run over and apologize a million times immediately, but I decided they might want space. And I kind of wanted space, too. Tiredness weighed me down, like something had drained me of any energy I had.

The whole van ride back to campus, I hardly heard a word anyone said to me. I pretended it was because my headphones were playing something, but truthfully I wore them just so people might leave me alone. Miss Noon patted my knee a few times from the seat beside me, like she felt sorry for me. And I didn't blame her. Who *wouldn't* pity someone who had to sit with a teacher because their best friends left no room for them? I wondered if this counted as regression—pushing myself back into solitude to think this whole thing over.

The newspaper clipping, the fire flash in my chest, my outburst . . . How did it all fit together? How was it connected to Mac and Mrs. Perrin?

. . . And why did I call myself "she"?

CHAPTER 28

That night and all the next day as I got ready for my first monthly slumber party in the rec room, I couldn't stop thinking about all the weird stuff happening to me. *Maybe we should do some digging.* Mac's words echoed as I pulled on my favorite pajama bottoms, covered in manatees on summer vacation. At least I could look at the Jet Skiing manatees and pretend I was having a good time. Slumber parties weren't in my mental scenario map, and I was a little worried about how it would go.

"I can always come back upstairs if I hate it," I told myself. Some of my sleep shirts seemed too uncool to consider wearing, so I tossed them onto my bed. "This isn't mandatory. It's supposed to be fun. And I can try and make things right with Ami while I'm there."

I grabbed my silk bonnet from my dresser. After shaking loose my jewelry, which I'd stashed inside during my shower, I stuffed my braids into my bonnet.

"And! Maybe I can ask other girls about anything weird they've seen," I said. Talking to myself aloud made me feel less nervous about being in our room alone. "I'll bring a notebook and write down any new information. Like a detective. A ghost detective. Ugh, why did I pack this shirt."

Nothing against *The Magic Shop*, but a kiddie show like that didn't exactly ooze cool points. And I didn't need anybody to know I still watched it. I tossed this shirt over near the other rejects. But it didn't land on my bed like it should have.

It stayed there, right in the middle of the air, draped as though I'd thrown it on a person's head. The shock of it froze me in place. I waited. And waited more. And eventually, I threw another shirt. This caught on the invisible body, too, like it had landed on a shoulder.

Vee had gone ahead of me to the rec room, so I couldn't call for her. In a horror movie, this would be the moment where the final girl left alive would grab a weapon and start yelling for the entity to face her. Or run away. But my brain couldn't process exactly how to make my limbs do *anything*, let alone do something smart.

". . . Mac?" Not smart. Extremely not smart. A second after I spoke, I regretted it. What did I expect to happen? "Okay. Okay, whatever is in the room, I'm not scared of you. And we already talked about this. Leave me alone."

The shape remained. My heart thumped in my ears. *Be brave*, I reminded myself. I wanted nothing more than to just grab a shirt and run. Instead, I backed my way toward my dresser. I kept my eyes on the shape as I patted my hand around to feel for my phone. Unlocking it without looking was simple; I was used to sneaking phone time at dinner or bedtime. A quick glance to open my camera, slowly raising it to frame the shape, and—

A knock at the door made me gasp. Ami poked their head into the room.

"Hey," they said softly. "Can we talk?"

I looked back at the shape, but my clothes had collapsed flat on the floor. My skin prickled. It took me a moment to get back to Ami, but eventually, I nodded.

They walked in with a sigh and bounced down onto Vee's bed. "I thought we could talk in private," they said, "before the slumber party. About what happened yesterday."

"I'm really sorry," I said. They looked surprised, but then smiled a little. "I don't know what happened. I . . . It felt like it wasn't me."

"Well, it didn't *sound* like you, either," Ami said. "I was talking to Vee about it and I'm not mad at you. I'm concerned. The haunting stuff . . . Maybe it's affecting you a lot more than it seems?"

"I don't know," I said. I slumped into my desk chair. "Maybe you're right. Something is wrong and I don't know how to fix it. But I'm trying to figure it out."

"Well . . . you don't have to figure it out alone," Ami said. They shrugged, then slung an arm around my shoulder. I leaned into the side hug almost out of desperation. "Whatever it is. Your brain overloading, ghosts, a demon . . . Whatever it is. I guarantee me and Vee gotcha."

I couldn't stop myself from bursting into tears. I had real friends at last.

CHAPTER 29

Once, in first grade, I threw up in front of the whole school. A stomach bug had been going around, and I started not feeling well during lunch. I didn't want to get in trouble for getting up when we weren't supposed to, so I thought I could wait for the bell to get up and go to the bathroom.

I couldn't.

Gross chunks of goo spilled out of my mouth, all over my lunch tray, my clothes, my shoes. Kids at my table started yelling and running away. I felt so embarrassed, I got sick again from the anxiety. That was the worst feeling I'd had in my whole school career.

After making up with Ami, I should've been relieved. I should've been happy. But somehow, standing together in the doorway of the dayroom where the slumber party was supposed to take place, I felt even worse than I did that day in first grade.

It was as if every bad emotion, every unpleasant feeling I'd ever felt was hanging over the room, heavy like a cloud. But it was like only I could feel it. The invisible entity in my room didn't seem so bad compared to this feeling of dread bearing down on me.

Nobody else gave any clue that they were uncomfortable. Conversations carried on, people set up sleeping bags, goofed around, whispered and whined and threw things at each other. Theo, Nicole, and Lily sat nearly center, exchanging face masks and nail polish. Everyone seemed just fine. And that made me feel even *less* fine.

Ami, wearing sparkly gold pajama pants and a crewneck with something written in huge Thai letters with a little Black resistance fist in a lower corner, nudged me with their elbow. "It's weird, right?" they said.

"What?"

"The vibes in here," they elaborated. "It's weird. Like something's about to happen."

My spine shivered. They nailed it with that description. I felt like whenever I rode those tall drop rides with Egypt at fairs. Like we were stuck at the top, waiting to be slammed back down to the ground. Any second, that drop was coming. And I couldn't prepare myself for it.

"I usually ignore it," they continued, shrugging. "It goes away eventually."

They pulled me along with them to the side of the room near an air hockey table, then rolled out their black sleeping bag next to Vee's. I didn't see her around, though, so she was probably in the bathroom. I frowned. We were pretty far from Theo, but I couldn't ask Ami to move. It's not like I wanted to be near Theo's friends, but I was starting to believe that Theo really did feel bad. So I plunked my stuff down and started to unfurl my own sleeping bag. "You feel it, too?"

"Sorry, your face was like—" They made an exaggerated scared face, growling goofily, and I couldn't help but smile a little. "I used to look like that when I first started going here. But eventually you just get used to it. You want a dumpling?"

I accepted the little lumpy dough ball, obviously, but couldn't make myself eat it right away. I listened to Ami talk about this one time that they had helped their dad make dumplings, and how their dog ate six of them and then pooped everywhere. But I couldn't really concentrate on that or move past the weird pre-drop feeling.

"How do *you* feel it and nobody else does?" I asked, even though they were in the middle of talking.

They stopped and thought for a moment. "I dunno." They

shrugged. "My granny says some people are just sensitive. Like me. Like, she says when I was little I'd talk about my life before this one. I used to be a cabaret dancer—isn't that cool?"

My cheeks got warm at that; I'd seen photos from MawMaw Septine's days as a dancer. Tiny sparkly costumes that showed off too many things I didn't wanna see on a grandma, even in younger pictures, huge elaborate headpieces, lots of dark makeup . . . I wasn't exactly sure what cabaret was, but I imagined it was similar. It was way too embarrassing to imagine grown-up old-timey Ami like that.

"I've always been taught that there's things we don't, or I guess *can't*, understand. Some people ignore it, some people stare it right in the face."

"And it doesn't scare you?"

"Oh no, it's *super* scary," Ami said, shaking their head. "But lots of things are scary. And nobody's ever died behind a weird feeling, right? People die from actions."

"When I asked you about the ghost—"

"I don't like talking about it too much in front of the others," they cut me off. "They're not like us. They don't feel things. Anyway, if you're not gonna eat that, *I* will."

I handed them the dumpling back just as Vee found us and made herself comfy.

Ami saw ghosts and spoke about it like it was nothing. Like they were talking about visiting family or their grades on a quiz. They saw ghosts, and they saw them here, and they weren't afraid. I wished I knew what that felt like. Anxiety made me afraid way too often, and autism made me struggle to explain just *why* I was afraid. I sighed and held my stuffed brontosaurus to my chest.

Someday, maybe. Someday I'd be brave like Ami.

CHAPTER 30

The slumber party felt chaotic in the best way. A movie played on the huge television, but not many people watched. I tried paying attention, to the movie and to my friends, but I couldn't shake the uneasy feeling. My headphones from Theo helped a tiny bit, but not as much as I'd hoped. But even so, it was nice that I could wear them without anybody telling me I was weird. No one mentioned them at all.

By the time the third movie started, I was yawning practically every other second. I could hardly keep my eyes open. But I refused to be the first to fall asleep. To keep myself from fully fading, I stood up. And that was a mistake.

Nicole sneered at me, arms folded, mouth moving. Lipreading was impossible for me, so I started to take off my headphones so I could hear her just as she rolled her eyes and walked off. A few other girls followed. Theo, in the nicest, fanciest purple silk pajama set I'd ever seen, hung back. She looked over her shoulder, then walked toward me.

"You don't have to come if you don't want to," she said. I still didn't know what was even happening. I looked to Ami and Vee. Vee seemed encouraging, giving me a thumbs-up, but Ami looked at Theo the way Nicole looked at me. I added a subgoal: have Theo and Ami get along.

"I can come," I said. Theo grinned and held a hand out to me. And for some silly reason, I took it. Ami and Vee both shook their heads resolutely and stayed behind.

We caught up to the others, and I regretted agreeing without knowing just what was happening. Everyone crowded into the upstairs bathroom, the place I'd first met Mac. And as soon as Theo and I entered, a girl from my biology lab closed the door. My throat tightened; too many people, too small a space. Deep breaths helped ward off my rising panic.

"We have to say it all at the same time," someone I didn't know said. The lights flicked off, and nervous chatter and uneasy laughs bubbled up. Someone turned on a few flameless candles. Theo smiled at me in the mirror, but I couldn't return the gesture. "Count of three. One. Two—"

Oh no.

They were trying to do some kind of Bloody Mary game.

I cussed at myself mentally for being so willing to blindly follow Theo.

"*Bloody Mary, I killed your baby!*

Bloody Mary, I killed your baby!

Bloody Mary, I killed your baby!"

And then silence. A few seconds passed, and a girl on the other side of the group began laughing. That made other girls laugh along with her. Even I managed a little smile. Expecting something to happen was ridiculous, of course. Bloody Mary had been played at sleepovers for years and no cases of someone showing up had ever been reported. Nothing to freak out over. Even though a small part of me still felt super *I don't play with demons.*

I hated mirrors in daylight. By candlelight, they were even creepier. I knew all about tricks brains played on people when they looked too long into mirrors. Facial features distorted. Eyes seemed like they melted. Reflections appeared rippling. The illusion made people think of hauntings or demons, because who likes thinking that it's just a visual trick of the brain?

But I kept staring like I didn't know any of that. Like something spooky really would appear any second and Mary just worked on Mary time. No blinking, just staring. I watched the candlelight dance among the shadows. And I counted.

Nine of us crammed into this bathroom. Ten people in the mirror.

I counted again.

And again.

And again.

Ten heads. When it should have been nine. And that made me want to make it eight.

I kept my eyes on this tenth head—the back of it faced away from the rest of us so all that was visible was dark, dark hair. The other girls chattered loudly; no one seemed to notice. The extra head began to turn. Slowly, slowly, slowly.

"Theo," I whispered. I knew she wouldn't hear me above everyone else. But my voice wouldn't get any louder. I cleared my throat to try again. "The—"

Someone screamed. And then, like dominoes, the other girls fell into screaming, too.

CHAPTER 31

Screams bled into howling laughter within seconds. I didn't understand it; didn't they see this extra girl? Weren't they just as scared as me?

Blame was tossed around about who started all the yelling. Friendly shouting, some nudging, teasing. But I couldn't join in. I could only stare at Mac.

Mac, in the mirror. The head that now faced forward. The eyes now staring right at me, *through* me. Her smirk felt violent even without her doing anything at all. My breathing turned shallow. Sweat slithered down my back. I felt hot. Way, way too hot.

"Eva?" That underwater sound came back as Theo spoke, and my sight narrowed to a pinprick. I knew by now this meant another vision was coming on. "Are you okay? What are you smiling at?"

"It's super hot in here," the girl from biology complained.

As others began agreeing, Mac reached a hand up and laid it on her chest. Without thinking, I mirrored her. But I didn't feel anything there—my locket was gone.

My shower. I forgot to put it back on after my shower.

Suddenly, each candle flame whooshed into a huge ball of fire. More screams. Just as soon as the flames grew, they all disappeared. We were surrounded by darkness. Smoke floated beneath the door. Whispers and screams came through the vents, voices that we didn't recognize.

"HELP ME!"

"WE'RE IN HERE!"

"HELP!"

"PLEASE LET US OUT!"

The smoke billowed upward, thick and hot and suffocating. I coughed and tried waving it away. The screaming pleas grew even louder. Someone slammed the door open. The others, unaffected by what I was seeing, screamed and laughed and raced out of the bathroom. But I couldn't take my eyes off Mac.

Not when she leaned forward.

Not when her hand reached toward me.

Not when she pulled herself right *out* of the mirror.

Mac fell from the counter. She landed in a crumpled heap at my feet. I leaped back just as her smoldering arm shot out to grab at my ankle. The towel rack jabbed right into my spine. I

145

didn't have a moment to feel it—Mac rose to her feet in a way that looked like a few frames of reality had been cut out. It was unnatural.

My hands fumbled in the dark for something, anything, to use as a weapon. Every step back was met with Mac stepping forward. She watched me with that deranged smile. Embers burned beneath her skin. Smoke billowed around her. Around me. Until we were only a few hairs' width apart.

"Now I can *make* you stay," she growled. I gagged from the scent of burned flesh overpowering me. "Let me in, Eva."

"Not a freaking chance!" I said.

Mac's charred jaw fell open. A piercing, impossibly loud scream came out of her. And I knew, somehow, that sound was coming out of me, too.

CHAPTER 32

My screams, Mac's screams, seemed to last centuries. The bathroom light clicked on. I whipped my head up to the ceiling, then over toward the light switch, where Theo stood, confused.

She looked scared of me.

I watched her mouth move but couldn't hear a word she said. I looked at the other girls crowding the bathroom door behind her. I glanced around for Mac and saw . . . no one. My stomach heaved. I felt dizzy.

"Just stop, Nicole," Theo was saying as I drifted back into reality. "I dunno what your deal is, but you're being ridiculous."

"So you'd rather hang out with this weirdo and the other crazies than with us?" Nicole said.

Down the hall, a scream. No, more like . . . a wail. Wailing that cut off all chatter outside the bathroom. As if silence might keep whatever it was out there away from us. The ones outside crowded back into the bathroom with me as the wailing grew closer, closer, closer. Until it was right outside the door. Theo squeezed my hand and I held hers just as tight.

"What the heck is happening?" she whispered.

I had no answer.

Pounding at the door joined the wailing. Heavy and urgent. Not just from one person hitting the door, either. It sounded as if dozens of hands banged away. The girls behind me started to scream, too. I could swear someone back there was crying. I wanted to scream and cry, too, but instead, I took a deep breath.

"Leave us alone!" I yelled so loud I felt like I blew out a vocal cord.

With one heavy release, the wailing stopped. The pounding faded. But my shoulders stayed hunched near my ears, tension keeping me in place. No one else moved, either. Decades passed in the next couple minutes of silence.

"Open the door," Nicole said in a quiet rush.

"*You* open it," a different girl responded.

No one stepped up to open the door. I started to move, but Theo kept me back. I really wanted to leave, though, to be anywhere but here. I stared at the door like I might be able to open it by thinking really hard.

And then, the door latch clicked.

The door creaked and cracked open.

None of us moved. For a few seconds, at least. Nicole shoved people out of the way and ran out, and several other kids were hot on her heels. Until only Theo and me remained. She watched me with worry, then dragged me out of the bathroom with her.

Downstairs, Theo grabbed her sleeping bag and brought it closer to mine. Ami sat up with an annoyed look. "Um, excuse you—"

"Not now, Ami," Theo said with a weary sigh.

Ami looked at Vee, then me. They raised an eyebrow.

"What happened up there?" Vee asked.

The other girls who had been upstairs were huddled together, talking hurriedly, but none of them had said anything to Miss Pixie. And if Miss Pixie had heard anything, she definitely wasn't letting on about it. Every few seconds, one of them looked to me as if what happened was somehow my fault.

Maybe it was.

"I think Mac is getting stronger," I said. "And I think it's got to do with the centennial festival."

"Holy crow," Vee gasped, just as Theo said, "Mac?"

"The ghost. I saw her upstairs. The girl from the newspaper."

"Newspaper?" Ami repeated.

"The one who looks like you?" Theo asked. I nodded. "Why would—"

"I dunno," I said. "But I want to find out. It doesn't make a lot of sense in my head yet, but . . . Maybe you guys can help me figure it out and put a stop to all of this."

Theo and Ami locked eyes for a few seconds. I half expected one of them to throw a pillow or tell me to get lost for even making them think about working together. But instead, Ami sighed and looked back at me with a small nod. I grinned; subgoal on the way to completion.

"Is the library still open?" I asked.

"For upperclassmen, yeah," Vee said. "But not anybody in lower grades."

Breaking rules was more Egypt's thing than mine. It stressed me out too much to go against authority. My brain always assumed the Rules Police would come out of the shadows and throw me straight into jail. Rules existed for a reason, and they made me feel safe and more aware of social conventions. But . . . rules failed to offer any guidance about being haunted.

I inhaled as deep as I could. "We gotta go to the library," I said, "and it's gotta be tonight."

I felt on the edge of my seat for the next hour. I didn't even really pay attention to Theo or Vee or even Ami trying to talk to me as we sat. Or really, I *couldn't*. My mind was a noisy place to begin with, like a bunch of TVs playing different things at different volumes all at the same time. But as we waited for lights out and Miss Pixie to go upstairs to her room, I only heard one thing. Mac, in my head, begging me to stay here at Blythe with her. Sometimes she whispered, sometimes it was a terrible growl. But always Mac, always telling me to stay.

Theo's fingers slid in between mine. It felt even better than the last time she held my hand. One of the brain TVs started playing a really sappy Karen Cooper song and my cheeks burned.

Or, maybe my cheeks *actually* burned. Because not long after, it felt like a thousand tiny flaming needles were stabbing through my palm. I felt bad for pulling away, but if Theo was upset, she didn't show it. I heard Mac's laughter cackling in my head. I felt my blood boil, and not because I was being messed with by a dead girl. Mac ruined my time with Theo and laughed about it.

Mac was going down.

CHAPTER 33

When the lights turned out, I lay down for only a second. Miss Pixie lived on the third floor; I tried counting in my head how long it might take her to get up there, get settled, and crawl into her bed. Twenty minutes seemed long enough. Some girls in the dayroom were already snoring a bit, so it probably meant we could slip out.

I nudged Ami and Vee with my foot. I grabbed my backpack and pulled out my clothes, leaving my sketchbook and some pens inside. That way, I could take notes on anything we found. We tiptoed out of the dayroom in turns, waiting a few minutes between each of us. And then we were outside, skulking through the night.

I wanted to throw up. The clock neared midnight and we were out of the dorm, walking through campus, breaking all kinds of rules. But more than that, I felt terrified that I might see the ghastly woman again. Or Mac. Or the shape. Or, heck, all of them. Maybe they were working together. Haunting together. Maybe they were all Mac in different forms. I grabbed Vee's hand to try and calm myself down a little. This was fine. We were fine. Just a quick trip to the library and then right back to our sleeping bags. Easy peasy.

The library was empty when we entered, but thankfully unlocked. The library felt massive, and old, and way fancier than other libraries I'd been to. Ami said it wasn't really that old—and a brick on the side of the door said EST. 1942—but they'd designed the library and the rest of the campus buildings to *look* like old colleges in Europe. Inside, arches and thick columns were everywhere. A bust of someone I couldn't recognize sat near the checkout desk. It felt like a movie library instead of a real one.

I followed Vee, Ami, and Theo into the archives room. We decided to split up the work: Ami looked for info on the building collapse, Vee searched for Mrs. Perrin, and Theo and me searched for Mac. Or Sutton.

So many pages came up when we looked for *Mac* and none of them were any use to us, so I switched my strategy to search for *Sutton* instead. This time, more relevant results came up. The text of the links talked about cotillions, birthdays, attending weddings of family members . . . I moved back up to the top of the page to work my way down.

The first link at the top was just a very short news article about the town's land purchased by the Friends of Lafayette Falls Lake. The article documented the cost of the sale and detailed how the sharecroppers had used the land. It mentioned a small general store, a bank, a doctor's office . . . but my attention was grabbed by the cemetery. I recognized the view from the angle of the photograph. It was almost the same view I saw every morning in homeroom. Except the land around was mostly empty. And, of course, homeroom didn't have any graves.

The caption under the photograph of the cemetery said *Eternal View Cemetery, established 1919, housed notable graves, such as Dr. Elson F. MacArthur (left), first Negro doctor in Overton Heights, and his young daughter, Sutton MacArthur (right).*

Their graves were hard to read, and zooming just made the already sorta fuzzy picture even blurrier. Now at least I had a full name. Sutton MacArthur. I backed out of that article to look at the second. This article, several years before the land sale, made my skin crawl. Instead of being from what was apparently the main newspaper for the area, the *Falls Gazette*, this was from the *Freedmen Flyer*. My grandparents, both sets, had talked to Egypt and me about freedmen. About slavery and sharecroppers and everything their—our—families went through just to live in peace. But it wasn't the source that made me uneasy. It was the headline.

MACARTHUR AND DAUGHTER DEAD! MURDER SUSPECTED

The two had been at his practice, closing up for the day. A fire broke out, and they were unable to escape. This had been the fifth fire in as many weeks, but the first to have casualties. The way the article was worded, it sounded as if many of the townsfolk suspected a certain unnamed group of setting these fires to run the sharecroppers out of their town. I felt sick. And confused— Mrs. Perrin had said nothing was on the land when the Friends established the school. But clearly there had been a whole thriving community.

Portraits of the doctor and his daughter ran along with the article, and I almost didn't believe it. But Mac smiled at me from the picture, hair plaited in two braids threaded with ribbon, wearing a clean, tidy version of that burned white dress I saw her in.

I already knew that Mac wasn't a student; she wasn't from this time. I knew we were somehow connected. But it was something else to find concrete proof. Mac—Sutton MacArthur—died over a hundred years ago.

She died because some bad people did bad things to people who were just trying to live their lives. She died in one of the worst ways I can imagine. So of course she was angry at the fake story told for years about the origins of the town. Destroying the school because of that rage seemed too much, but on some level . . . I understood. The things I'd been experiencing started to click. The smoke, the burn mark, the charred look Mac appeared with. It all had to do with this fire that took the lives of Mac and her father. My heart broke for them. And in some part, for every Black American. I knew this wasn't the first, last, or only time tragedy like this happened and was forgotten. Covered up. Erased.

Nobody deserved that. No matter how scary they were.

What I still didn't understand, though—how could Mac have appeared in photographs printed alongside the building collapse article if she'd already died decades before it happened?

CHAPTER 34

I scribbled details about the article into my sketchbook and printed off as much as I could. Heat rippled under my skin with every stroke of my pencil. Whether it was Mac or me, I didn't know, but so much anger pulsed in me that I thought my head might pop. Sutton MacArthur, Mac, died in a fire and was buried in a cemetery that used to be beneath the school's foundation. And she wanted me to join her.

What did that even mean? Maybe that was why Mac was stuck here—they must have moved her body without her spirit following along.

"Look at this." I kept my voice quiet while I plunked the stack of printed articles on the table we had claimed. Vee gasped. Ami and Theo both reached for the top sheet. Theo drew back, though, and let Ami have it.

"Holy crow, this does look like you," Ami commented. They

looked back and forth between the paper and me, then passed the sheet to Theo.

I dove into my next hunch. Mac, Mrs. Perrin, the ghostly voices, the shape—all of it had to do with this cemetery. They were stuck here, stuck roaming around campus scaring the pants off students. They wanted their cemetery back, and they wanted us to pay for taking it away. So maybe if we found out the new location of the cemetery and helped them reconnect with their remains, all these creepy things would stop. No more smoke or screams or surprise visits from Mac.

All the while, I fought against so many different urges. I wanted to fling the papers all over the place to stop my friends from reading them. I wanted to kick and scream and throw chairs. I wanted to *hurt*. But it wasn't really me. I wasn't going to let Mac's rage overtake me. I had the tools to calm myself, to keep myself mostly level. Using them against a ghost wasn't much different from using them during a meltdown.

Since Ami knew extra records that hadn't been scanned yet were stored upstairs, we made our way up a winding staircase to find them.

"I've only been up here once," Ami said as we climbed. They slid their hand along the railing and I watched their glittery nails sparkle. "I got to help sort some stuff last summer. It kinda smells up here. Like old socks and stale coffee."

As soon as we got closer, I understood what they meant. That musty closet smell spread all over the place up here. Piles of books, their spines broken and covers hanging on by a thread, littered the floor. We barely had room to walk through. The deeper we went, the more closed-in everything felt. My chest started to tighten even though normally, I didn't mind tight spaces. Mama, unlike me, definitely would have run off already.

Voices caught my attention, and I stopped. It sounded like a melody, a quiet song that someone was trying to keep to themselves. I stepped super lightly to go figure out where the sound was coming from. A door to the left was open slightly, and when I leaned in, I could hear singing.

Well. More like chanting.

A lifetime of sneaking into Egypt's room taught me how to open a door as quietly as possible. I poked my head in, just barely, to see if anyone was standing close by. Not seeing anyone, I looked in more, then stepped in halfway. The voices started to sound kinda familiar, and I turned to look at Theo, who shrugged before grabbing on to my pajama shirt's hem.

We crept deeper in, and I noted how bare and dusty this room was. But just around the other side of a wall near the door, things looked totally different. Candles and lanterns covered just about every space—some unlit and whole, others burned down to the base of the wick. A huge table sat dead center, with a bloodred tablecloth covering it. On top of the table, more books, more trinkets, some goblets, a huge vaselike bottle with something dark inside.

Around the table, chant-singing in a language I didn't recognize, were teachers I *did* recognize—Miss Noon, Miss Gloriana, Miss Eugenie . . . and Miss Alice.

Behind me, Ami gasped and backed up a few steps. Their shoes hit the creakiest floorboard in the world, and the chanting immediately stopped. All four women whipped their heads round to look at us, and my blood turned to ice.

Miss Noon looked as if we'd walked in on her doing something embarrassing. Eyes wide, mouth dropped open, shoulders tense. She immediately tossed down the paper she had been holding on to, taking a step back from the table. Miss Gloriana and Miss Eugenie both glared at us. I could hear Miss Gloriana cursing in Spanish as she started to cover something up on the table. But Miss Alice . . .

Her mouth tightened into a wrinkly pucker. Candle flames flickered in her eyes and made her look . . . well, evil. She took a few slow steps closer to us. Immediately, I knew what we had to do to keep safe.

"*RUN!*"

CHAPTER 35

Books flew all over the place as we knocked into them trying to run for our lives. An atlas from the 1700s almost murdered me, but I caught myself, scraping my hands on the floor, and went right back to running. Down the stairs, through the lobby, straight out the library, and back to the dorm. We didn't stop or slow down until we got to Clearwater.

"What the hell was that!" Ami shout-whispered, panting and pressing against the back of my dorm room door.

"Heck," I said.

"Whatever, what just happened?!"

I didn't have an answer. We'd stumbled on four of our teachers doing something that looked a heck of a lot like summoning a spirit or trying to raise the dead. There was no way that that's what they were doing, though. Was it? Why *would* they be? Unless . . .

"That was definitely something dark sided," Vee piped up.

She'd buried herself within her comforter. "And now they know that we know. We're boned."

"We didn't see anything." Theo, cross-legged on my bed, tried to comfort us. "And they didn't really see our faces. I think we'll be fine."

"Miss Noon recognized me," I mumbled. No one said anything. Oh no. I'd ruined all my friendships. I scrambled to save things. "But . . . it's okay, she's nice. She's a family friend. She wouldn't hurt any of us."

"That's what they *want* you to think." Ami sat down next to Theo. I wanted to be happy that my subgoal got kicked up a notch, but my stomach just ached at the thought of getting pushed out of the group for this. "I've seen all sorts of true crime shows. I know how it goes."

"The call always comes from inside the house," Theo said.

"Most crime is committed by people you know," the blanket mass of Vee agreed with a nod.

I sighed. My hands almost immediately started to squish my stuffed brontosaurus as I desperately sought out some kind of comfort. Normally, I could rely on my headphones or my sketchbook or a squishy kitty toy I kept in my bag but—

Oh crap.

"My bag!" I gasped.

Vee immediately uncovered herself. Theo and Ami both had wide eyes as they stared at me.

"Oh crap," Ami said. "Ohhh crap."

"We have to go back," I told them as I stood.

"*Do* we, though . . . ?" Vee asked.

I wanted to agree with her and say my stuff was just lost to the library forever. But I couldn't let my sketchbook go. Ami insisted they wouldn't step back in there, which meant I would have to go on my own. Which made it even more tempting to just abandon my stuff.

I checked the time on my phone. It was 1:39 a.m. How could I possibly get into the library and get my bag without being caught by the teachers? Knowing the teachers might find my bag before I could get it back made my urge to throw up almost become reality.

Calm breathing helped enough that we could decide to solve the problem in the morning and all say good night. I managed to get to sleep eventually.

In the morning, I woke up just before breakfast service for students began in the dining hall. I could sneak into the library, grab my bag, and rush out. Then I could creep off campus, do some more research in town, and avoid having to be interrogated by Miss Noon or anyone else.

I pulled my hair into a low ponytail and tucked it inside my hoodie, then slid on a cap I borrowed from Daddy some years ago and hadn't given back yet. Maybe no one would recognize me underneath a Royals cap if they couldn't see my braids. Better still, I grabbed my sunglasses and slid those on, too, then turned to leave the room.

Theo, in Vee's bed, was sitting up staring at me. I yelped and jumped back. Vee snored a little and rolled over.

"Sorry!" Theo said as she scooted out of my way. I must have been so exhausted last night that I hadn't realized that she stayed in our room instead of going down to her own room. It was almost unfair how pretty she was—even at such an early hour, even after just waking up. And with her eyes wide in surprise, she looked like a painting.

"I heard you moving around," she said. "Breakfast?"

"Um . . . the library," I mumbled. "I have to get my bag."

Theo nodded. "You look like you're on the run from the FBI."

The flutters in my stomach bubbled upward to make me smile. I wanted to fill her in on my half-baked plan. I wanted to invite her to come along with me so we could solve this together like a movie. But I didn't.

"I gotta go," I blurted, just before bolting out into the hall.

CHAPTER 36

I hadn't walked five feet out of Clearwater before I ran into Miss Pixie on her way back from breakfast. My stomach fell into my sneakers. She grinned at me with that peppy cheerleader smile.

"Good morning, sweetheart," she chirped. "Love the hat! Kansas City, right?" I hummed. "Yeah, go Chiefs!" Mama, a through and through Saints fan, would've booed loudly at that. "I'm a football girlie, but my wife *loves* baseball. We're both super into KC's teams, though! She's from Overland Park. Oh, where's your locket? I don't think I've ever seen you without it."

I clutched my throat. Oh no. Why did I keep forgetting to put my necklace back on? I normally wore it every day.

I heard an echo of a laugh in the back of my mind . . . It was Mac, getting into my head again. It made me shiver—it was disturbing for my mind to not be my own.

Miss Pixie clearly didn't actually want an answer. She kept talking: "If you hurry up, you'll still have time to go get it."

She was right—going back and getting my locket would give me something to hold on to during the day when I felt anxious. I considered heading back to my room and just staying there, but the thought of staying in my room alone seemed worse than whatever the teachers might have in store for me. So I sighed, nodded, and hustled upstairs to clasp the locket around my neck before hurrying to the academic building.

When I walked into homeroom, Miss Eugenie was in there, talking to Miss Gloriana and Miss Noon in hushed tones. They grew quiet once Miss Gloriana noticed me. The staring felt awkward, and their eyes followed me as I sat down. I stole a quick look at Miss Eugenie, and she was watching me the way my grandma Nanay's cat watched birds from the screened-in porch. I pretended not to notice.

Seconds before the bell rang, the other two teachers finally left. I busied myself with tracing shapes on my desk, drawing with nothing but my finger, and praying that Miss Noon would leave me alone.

"Eva, a moment please?" Miss Noon said. I winced. So much for my attempt to hide. A suspension was definitely on the way. Or worse.

I walked up to her desk, and she motioned for me to walk around it to get even closer. She slid a candy bowl toward me, but I shook my head. She gave me a smile, but not the normal one. This one looked like she was maybe standing on a tack.

"So, I heard you made a little after-hours trip to the library yesterday," she said. "And that you may have seen something a little scary."

I had. Teachers standing around a table singing in some unknown language was definitely terrifying. And she already knew I'd seen it. I kept quiet the way we're taught to do in front of cops. I wasn't about to rat myself out.

Once she realized I wasn't going to say anything, she continued. "I want you to know you can talk to me about anything," she said. "And I want you to understand that sometimes we *think* we see things that might not really be there."

"I don't know what you mean." My voice shook, but at least I used it.

A frustrated sigh fell from Miss Noon's lips. "Eva . . ."

"What you're doing is called gaslighting," I said. I wasn't entirely sure I was using that word the right way, but it got Miss Noon's attention. She was supposed to be my safe person. How could she do this to me? "Dr. Choudhury taught it to me. If I saw something, and I'm not saying that I did, but *if* I did—it was as real as you and me talking right now. And Auntie Nooncie would never try to make me think I imagined something when I didn't. So I don't understand why Miss Noon is."

I noticed myself shaking. I was so, so scared of what might happen to me after saying all that. I could almost *see* Miss Noon's heart breaking. But instead of blowing up at me, she just . . . stared.

She's afraid of you. Mac, quiet until now, hissed in my head. I swatted around my head as if that might chase her off. More than anything, I hated hearing her internally, hated the access she had to my mind. I needed to add that to my list of weird stuff to solve.

The bell rang again. "I have to go to class," I said. I took steps toward the door, but Miss Noon gripped my wrist to stop me from leaving.

"Just . . . be careful, Eva. Okay?"

It sounded like a threat. But maybe it was a warning? Either way, I didn't wait to find out. I nodded quickly and hurried to my next class. Not that I was heading anywhere better—I didn't want to see Miss Gloriana, either.

I waited until the very last second to walk into Miss Gloriana's classroom, right after Theo. Not that I was waiting for her, or only went in because of her. It just happened to be when the bell was about to ring. I sat close to the door, and she sat in front of me. She turned around and smiled for a second, and I started to smile back before it hit me. Miss Gloriana wasn't at the front of the classroom.

But Miss Alice certainly was.

CHAPTER 37

"Miss Gloriana has a personal matter to attend to," Miss Alice said. The entire class was silent; maybe *everyone* was scared of her, not just me. "I'll be watching you for the period. You may speak quietly. Any rowdy behavior and you'll be sent to my office. Am I heard?"

"Yes, Miss Alice," we all said at the same time.

After some hesitating, people started to chat in small groups. I desperately wanted my sketchbook. My nerves practically tripled every minute that passed without me being able to go fetch my bag. I just knew any second one of the teachers was going to pop up with a loud *GOTCHA!* and the four of us would be . . . expelled? Sacrificed?

"Miss Mauberry." Miss Alice curled a gnarled finger to summon me. I gulped.

The other kids got quiet once more, like if they said anything they'd get called up, too. Theo looked up at me as I stood. She gave my pinkie a quick squeeze with her own. While it didn't help me not be terrified of what was coming, I could be certain I had someone on my team. Even if that team would probably need to be pallbearers at my funeral.

As soon as I got near the desk, Miss Alice cleared her throat loudly. I stopped.

"Are you missing something?" Miss Alice asked. I couldn't tell if she knew already or was genuinely wondering. So I said nothing.

Seconds later, she lifted something from beneath the desk. It rested on the tip of her index finger. Purple, beat-up, kind of dirty, little black flashlight dangling from the strap.

My backpack.

I broke out in a sheen of sweat. She still didn't speak, and I very nearly confessed everything just to fill the silence. But I held it together.

"You continue to disobey very simple, explicit rules, Miss Mauberry," Miss Alice said quietly, just low enough for none of the other students to hear. "What, precisely, were you and your little group doing at the library during a time in which you should have been in your dorm?"

"I—"

"Think *extremely* carefully before you answer."

I tried to cast a look to Theo, but Miss Alice snapped her

fingers in my face. I saw red; snapping at people was so *rude*, so *snooty*. Like she didn't think of me as a real person. And maybe she didn't.

"You shouldn't snap at people," I said. Miss Alice's pointy eyebrow arched upward. "I can take responsibility for snooping, but I think *you* should apologize for snapping. It's not nice."

I took my bag strap and lifted it off her finger slowly while she glared daggers into me.

"Thank you for returning my bag," I said. She continued her imitation of a statue. After a long beat, I moved to return to my seat.

"What you saw," Miss Alice practically growled before I could move out of earshot, "is to be forgotten, as surely as this conversation will be. Understood?"

Understood. But not even remotely respected.

CHAPTER 38

"So I was thinking," I said as I poked at my chicken Caesar salad.

The three of us—Ami, Vee, and me—sat at our usual lunch table. I wanted to eat, but being so nervous made it difficult. Plus my salad had onions thrown in and I hated onions. I kept thinking about my bag and Miss Noon and talking back to Miss Alice. Miss Alice had to be waiting to punish me, right? If she'd gotten so upset about me just having a meltdown, then breaking curfew, sneaking around, and spying on whatever weird ritual they were doing had to have been a mega-violation.

"We know the teachers are up to something," I continued. "And maybe that *something* has to do with the ghosts. It's super strange that they threatened me but we haven't actually gotten in trouble."

"Maybe they're gonna suspend us during the centennial thing," Vee said.

"Maybe they'll burn us at the stake," Ami added on. They were doing the one-up thing again. It amused me, but it honestly wasn't the time.

"We have to go back," I blurted.

They stopped talking and stared at me. Heck, even *I* wanted to stare at me. I liked having time to prepare for doing things. *Needed* it a lot of the time. We'd avoided getting in trouble for now. None of us got hurt during our snooping. And I knew that Mac and I had some kind of connection. That should have been enough for me for now. But it wasn't.

"I mean. If what I'm thinking is right," I said, my voice shaking only slightly less than my leg, "then we don't have a whole lot of time to figure this out. The centennial celebration is in a couple days. Which means we've realistically got just one day to stop anything bad from happening. Which also means . . . we gotta go back to the records room."

"Okay, but that sounds scary, though," Vee said.

"Sure, but we need to know what they were doing up there," I argued. "If they're controlling the ghosts, or summoning them or something. And there could be more information about Mac and the cemetery in those unscanned files."

Vee's eyes got wide and she looked at Ami for backup. I almost expected Ami to agree; they hadn't wanted to return to get my bag, after all. But they nodded.

"We need to know," they said. "If they're gonna threaten us the way they have today, then we at least oughta have dirt to make us worthy of those threats, right?"

"Y'all, I really don't know about this." Vee frowned.

"The resident staff do a bingo thing," Ami said as they held Vee's hand. "Every Monday evening, from 5:30 to around ten or so."

". . . So they wouldn't be at the library," I said. We were on the same wavelength, and I felt good about that. "We can take pictures of things we find and then get back to the dorms before anybody notices we're gone."

Ami gasped. "Ooh, we could use a Ouija board in there to see if we can make contact with Mac or any of the other ghosts."

My whole body shivered when they mentioned a Ouija board. MawMaw Septine had one, and Egypt and I tried using it with her once. She talked to us about the history of spirit boards and how different groups would use different materials to talk to spirits. But she also warned us that they could be dangerous. That we could accidentally call forward things we had no business calling. When we used it years ago, something spelled out Egypt's name and said I was cursed. I never wanted to touch another spirit board ever again.

This time, Vee and I both objected. Ami waved our concerns off.

"The trouble will be getting a board," they continued. "But we could always make one."

"I have one." Theo showed up out of nowhere and made all three of us jump. I smiled at her, but Ami looked ready to fight. Their fist balled up at their side, and I took their hand to get them to try and relax. "Sorry. Not to eavesdrop. I just . . . I have a board, if you wanna use it."

"Don't you get tired of sneaking up on people?" Ami asked.

"It's a hobby of mine, actually," Theo said with a roll of her eyes. "Listen, I dunno why you need a board, but if you want one, I have one. But I want in on whatever you're doing."

"Okay," I said before Ami could say whatever rude thing I knew was about to come out of their mouth. I tried to give them a *trust me* look but wasn't sure I pulled it off. "Meet us back at the library at six."

"Eva," Ami hissed.

"Sure," Theo said with a nod. She smiled at me. "See you at six."

When she spun to leave, the air turned to vanilla and cherry. Of course she smelled like the best scents. Ami pulled their hand from mine.

"What was that!" they asked.

"She just wants to help," I said. I finally took an onion-free bite of my salad. "Why don't you and Theo get along?"

They growled a little, probably annoyed at me for even asking. "She and her friends are just so . . ."

176

"Mean?" Vee guessed.

"Mean," Ami agreed. "I don't like mean people. They pick on kids for no reason, and I don't want anything to do with anybody like that."

I frowned; Theo had been mean to me, sure, but . . . she was trying. People deserved to try and be something different.

"She hasn't hung out with Nicole lately. And you saw last night, she was pretty nice. You even kinda got along. Can't you just . . . keep doing that?" I asked. "It would mean a lot to me if you two at least tried to be friends."

"I guarantee nothing," Ami said. But they smiled, and I smiled back.

"The school collapsed on the fiftieth anniversary celebration," I reminded them. "And I have a bad feeling something will happen again on the one hundredth anniversary. So we better ask whatever spirits talk to us tonight what we can do to stop it."

CHAPTER 39

The wind blew way too hard that evening as we tried to make our way back to the library after dinner, leaning into the gale to keep our balance. Like it wanted to push us back into the dorm and abandon this investigation.

Vee was the most freaked out, so she volunteered to stay outside the library, armed with a walkie-talkie just in case the teachers showed up. Ami and I would meet up with Theo, go to the records room, and try to contact the school's ghosts. Easy peasy.

When we finally entered the library, I immediately spotted Theo sitting at a table close to the entrance. But she wasn't sitting alone. Lily sat right beside her, smiling and laughing. My stomach knotted.

"Hey!" Theo greeted us cheerfully and stood with her backpack. Lily got up, too. "I brought Lils. She's better with this thing than me."

"Hi," Lily said gently. Ami and I exchanged looks, and I could tell they thought this might be a trap, too. "Sorry for just showing up. Theo told me everything. She's right that I, uh, have been too hard on you. Sorry about that."

"Let's go," Ami said, cold and uninterested. I didn't know if I could trust what Lily was saying, so I stayed quiet.

We got upstairs to find it had been tidied up a little since we'd run through. Most students studied downstairs, so this area of the library was completely empty. Nothing was organized, but at least the path was cleared. The door to the room with the giant table—the witching room, Ami decided to call it—was closed this time.

"Locked," Ami said with a sigh. They felt around the pocket of their teddy-bear-like hoodie before pulling out a tool I wasn't familiar with. Kneeling, they pushed the tool into the lock and began jiggling it around.

". . . Why am I not surprised you know how to pick locks?" Theo asked, which got a small laugh out of Lily.

"Because you're an a—"

"Where'd you get that?" I asked a little louder than I really needed to, considering we were in a library.

"A lady never reveals her secrets," Ami grunted while they fought with the lock.

Seconds later, a little *click* sounded, and they pushed the door open with a quiet cheer. The room looked as disorganized as before, maybe even a little creepier with nobody in there. Theo immediately approached the giant table and plunked her backpack on top of it. She slid the Ouija board out, arranged the planchette on top, then started to look around. Ami, meanwhile, stacked a few books to prop the door open so we wouldn't get locked inside.

"It smells bad in here," Lily said nervously as she stopped, tugging on the edge of a photo that had halfway slipped out of a folder.

I moved closer to her and looked over to see the picture, too. I recognized it a little—it looked like the pictures I'd found at the general store and in the articles I'd printed. This one showed a big group of white men standing on the grounds, cemetery in the background. They held shovels and sledgehammers and wore hats and shielded their eyes from the sun. In front of them, laid on the ground like a kill on a hunting trip, were two busted-up gravestones. I leaned in to read the names as best I could—and gasped.

MacArthur. It *had* to be Mac and her dad.

My mouth grew heavy with spit that I couldn't swallow, like right before throwing up. Why would they photograph smashing a little girl's gravestone? This time, my anger was one hundred percent my own. The level of disrespect it took to wreck memorial markers . . . I wanted nothing more in the moment but to find a time machine and go back to punch all these men in the guts.

I couldn't stand to look at it any longer. Instead, I approached Ami as they rummaged through some papers stacked on the table. They glanced at me before going back to the papers.

"So far, nothing seems that interesting," they said. "But I dunno what any of this means."

I sat down and grabbed some papers and scrolls to go through myself. Like Ami said, a lot just looked like nonsense to me. But after digging a few minutes, I stopped. I double-checked. Triple. And then I laughed quietly.

"Jackpot."

CHAPTER 40

I had found a map. A clear indication that the Friends ruined the community that stood on this spot on purpose.

The map had two parts—one thicker layer underneath labeled OVERTON HEIGHTS and over that, paper-thin enough to see through, was labeled RIKER'S BEND MOCK-UP. The thin layer was the same shape as the town beneath, but with a much different layout. This had to be the Friends' plans for the land. It was fascinating, but I was drawn more to the notes that had been rolled up with the map.

I sat on the floor to start flipping through them. A few pages mentioned appraisals, and one had a list of dates and offers given to the sharecroppers, and how those sharecroppers had ultimately turned the Friends down. One page, though, made me pause. This page listed building names, dates, and a column for check marks. Some rows had dots next to them, and they didn't seem to have an obvious purpose.

As I scanned the list, I found something that tied it all together for me.

Office of Dr. EFM 11/2

EFM . . .

Oh no.

"Guys, I think—"

Before I could finish, thunder cracked loudly enough that the whole library vibrated. Theo jumped. Lily started to scream, but Ami clapped a hand over her mouth. It lasted an uncomfortably long time, like the thunder was warning me not to speak about what I found. But once it stopped, I kept going.

"I think the Friends set the fire that killed Mac," I said. Tears started stinging my eyes. I blinked them away to keep calm.

"The who?" Lily and Theo both said.

I stood and handed the papers to Ami. "The Friends of Lafayette Falls Lake," I said. "They bought the land, they built this town."

"Oh right, yeah, we learned about them during orientation," Lily said.

"Right." I nodded. "But there was a town here already—Overton Heights. Sharecroppers settled here. They got lucky enough to buy land and build lives here. And I guess the Friends wanted this land badly enough that they'd burn people alive to get it."

"For what?" Theo wondered. "There's nothing here."

"Do colonizers really need a reason to do what they do?" Ami asked.

Another huge thunder boom. This time, Theo jumped closer to me, close enough that our arms brushed. I almost forgot to be scared as the electricity from that touch went through me.

"We gotta hurry," Ami said. "The rain isn't here, but it's coming. If we're going to use the Ouija board, we should do it soon."

CHAPTER 41

"You have to touch the planchette really lightly," Lily told us after she finished her protection prayer and we dropped each other's hands. Her tía taught her, she'd said, and I kind of wanted to ask more, to see if her aunt was like my grandma. But I held it in; we had to get on with the show. "That way everybody knows you're not the one moving it."

Another crash of thunder. We'd mostly stopped jumping, but I felt Theo's shoulder press into mine. I barely realized I leaned in to meet her. My hands weren't sweaty, but they *were* shaking as I touched the little piece of plastic that, in theory, the ghosts would use to communicate with us. I hoped Theo wouldn't notice and think I was a baby.

Lily led us through the process of opening the board, of inviting spirits in. She didn't seem as jumpy or nervous doing this, and it was a little funny—something that most people would be freaked out by actually made her calm and confident. People were weird like that.

"Is anyone here with us?" Lily asked. Nothing happened.

Rain outside started pounding against the roof. A steady drip started to come down on the other side of the room, which explained why there was a random bucket there.

"Does anyone want to talk to us?" Lily tried to ask in a different way. Still nothing. She frowned. "Hello?"

"*Heeeeeelllllllllloooooooooooooo?*"

All three of us drew our hands off the board at that. Someone spoke, slow and whispery and deep. And it wasn't any of us.

Lily took a deep breath. "Okay . . . If you wouldn't mind, could you answer some questions for us?" she asked.

We waited for another voice to come through, or for the planchette to begin moving to spell out a response. Silence.

The witching room had a draft, but nervous sweat glued my shirt to my back. I could hardly breathe. The air felt thick, burning. If this was even a fraction of what Mac felt in her final moments, I couldn't imagine the actual agony of being burned alive.

"How many spirits haunt this campus?" Lily asked.

Nothing.

"Can you tell us how you died?"

Still nothing.

"What do you want from me?" I asked before Lily could get another question out.

The planchette jerked, just barely. It shimmied slow as molasses over to the S. Ami accused Theo of moving it, but we all denied moving it on purpose.

S. T. A. Y.

Stay.

I shuddered, imagining I felt the brush of a hand against the back of my neck. But then something metallic slipped off me and landed in the center of the board.

Another lightning strike lit the whole room. My breathing stopped.

Right there, right in the center of the Ouija board, was my locket.

"What the hell?" Ami asked.

"Heck," I whispered. I reached out and pinched the chain between my thumb and index finger. I pulled it closer slowly. The longer I held the necklace, the hotter I got.

Another puzzle piece locked in my brain. This necklace, somehow, hurt Mac. She had stopped me from remembering to wear it before. She was probably responsible for undoing the clasp, and now she was heating the metal so I'd want to drop it.

But I didn't. I tossed it back over my head quick as I could. But the second it touched my chest, I screamed. A horrible, growling scream that I'd never done—or even heard—before. Like I had two voices in me. Maybe two whole people. My spine twisted and twitched. I jerked and crashed to the floor. Around me, I could sort of hear the others yelling and panicking. But I couldn't respond. I couldn't stop bending and flexing and stretching my body as I wailed. It was like someone else's pain was being channeled through me.

As suddenly as the pain started, it stopped. Frozen, I slumped forward as I was lifted into the air, my tiptoes just barely brushing the wood beneath. I teetered and wobbled like someone was holding me up by my armpits. I did all I could to focus, to push out whatever was trying to control me, and I locked eyes with Theo, who was terrified. Guilt struck me, as if I was doing this to myself, to my friends, on purpose.

"Tell the truth," something deep in me rasped. A split second later, I crumpled to the floor.

CHAPTER 42

For a moment, I saw stars. The tears I tried to fight off earlier easily won the war.

Theo and Ami ran to me. Ami cupped my face while I sobbed. They asked a bunch of questions about how I felt but I couldn't answer a single one. I heard Lily talking but couldn't tell if it was to me or not.

The walkie-talkie in Ami's pocket clicked to life.

"Guys?" Vee said through the walkie-talkie. "Is everything okay in there? Cuz it's kinda weird out here . . ."

Ami scrambled to grab the walkie-talkie. "Vee! We need you to get help. Eva's hurt."

"What?"

"Eva needs hel—"

"Ami, is th . . . ou? I ca . . . but . . . okay?"

I managed to stand up with Theo's help as Ami started smacking the walkie. "Vee!" they shouted. "I can't hear you!"

"Are you pressing the right button?" Theo asked.

"*Yes* I'm pressing the ri—Vee!" Ami screamed again. "What is wrong with this stupid thing."

"Ami," I said. I knew I wasn't loud enough. Even without all the thunder, with all the pain pulsing through me I couldn't speak above a whisper.

I could breathe again, but only barely. I couldn't wrap my head around what had just happened to me. I was no longer burning from the inside, and I didn't hear Mac in my head.

Not just that, but all of a sudden the storm outside just stopped. But none of this felt positive. Instead, I prepared myself for something coming. And I didn't have to wait very long.

As I slogged my way toward the Ouija board, the air turned frigid. My shallow breath came like a soft, thin cloud. I thought about what had happened the last time I felt this way. My stomach turned.

I looked to see if the others were frozen like my homeroom classmates had been, but they weren't. They were puffing out ragged breaths, confusion passing among them. Theo held on to Lily's arm and leaned against her for warmth. This was all wrong. Again.

And then, all of a sudden, Theo was yanked away from us.

CHAPTER 43

Theo's fingernails scraped against the floor as she struggled to crawl away from the invisible force that was trying to drag her into the darkest corner of the room. She'd slid at least ten feet away in the blink of an eye. Lily was screaming, Ami shouting for Theo and running over to try and catch her. I felt sick as Theo was enveloped in shadows. And I still couldn't speak loud enough to help call to her.

Everything after happened nearly at the same time.

Ami fell the way Theo had, but this time I could see them being pulled along. Their body left a track in the dust as they were pulled, kicking and yelling and trying to punch whatever had them. But that was the problem—it looked like *nothing* had them.

Lily flew up into the air like a marionette. Her slip-on shoes clattered to the floor and kicked up more dust. And then she, too, was surrounded in shadows, hidden from my view.

That left just me. Alone.

I summoned all my strength and ran for the door, but the books propping it open had scattered and the door had slammed shut. It refused to budge. My eyes started to well with tears, my hands slamming furiously against the wood. I didn't even care about getting in trouble—I just wanted to get out. I just wanted to save my friends.

"*Eva* . . ."

I debated not turning around. I knew if I did, Mac would be there. What I didn't know was if it would be the Mac I knew, the kid with beat-up shoes and a sneaky smile, or the scary, angry girl with burns and a dirty white dress. My tears slid down my cheeks as I squeezed my eyes closed.

"Please," I said. Relief flooded me—I could speak again! But I couldn't think of anything more to say than to try and beg for . . . for what? To be let go? To get my friends back?

Laughter echoed throughout the witching room. I practically melted into the door as I tried to get as much space between me and Mac as possible. Somehow, I knew this was the end. I'd never see Egypt, or Daddy, or Mama, or any of my new friends again. I'd never get the cat my parents promised me for my thirteenth birthday.

I'd never get a thirteenth birthday.

My legs buckled at the thought. I fell to the floor, sobbing. More laughter, evil and deep, shook me to the bones. I watched a couple of candles on the table fall over. The tablecloth caught fire without hesitation. Flames cascaded down toward the floor, all over the stacks of paper, the map, the books. It slithered toward me almost mockingly. The air heated up, transforming the room into a smoke-filled trap in seconds.

Goodbye, Eva.

CHAPTER 44

I watched the fire engulf everything before me through blurry eyes. I gripped my locket tightly. I thought of my grandmother. My amazing, bold, fearless MawMaw Septine. I wanted to apologize for not living up to her legacy. For being so scared of life, people, and my own voice for so long. I knew she would be proud of me, anyway, for at least trying to speak up. But it felt like I hadn't done enough.

Or . . . maybe I had. Maybe I was too hard on myself. She'd tell me I was on my own path, at my own pace. And, more importantly right that moment, that the light in me grew stronger every time I used my voice. And right now, my light shined almost as bright as the fire surrounding me.

The fire.

How had it not swallowed me whole already?

I cracked an eye open and took a look around. The fire stopped just short of crawling up my pants. With one hand still gripped tightly to my locket, I reached out to it. Braced myself for burned fingertips. But . . . nothing. The fire surrounded my fingers, kept flickering violently. But nothing burned.

"Haints can't hurt me," I whispered. MawMaw Septine had been right. "Holy crow. Mac." I scrambled to my feet. "Maaaaaaaaaaaaaaaaac!" I screamed like I really was being burned. "Give them back to me! *Right* now!"

From the darkness on the other side of the room, where my friends had disappeared, Mac stepped out into the flames. Her eyes glowed just like fire. The burning embers within her seemed to be brighter than ever.

"Why are you doing this to me?" I asked. "What can I give you to get my friends back? You want me to stay, I'll stay. I'll stay forever if that's what it takes. Just please don't hurt them."

Mac pointed to my chest. The locket.

"Y-you want this?" I reached up to unclasp it but froze. I'd worn it for years, as long as I could remember. And the moment I forgot it, Mac had slipped into my mind. And when I'd put it back on over the Ouija board, she was already inside my head and it had hurt her terribly. The locket had been a gift from MawMaw Septine—there must be something about it keeping me safe. She wanted me to take it off so she could get back in again. "If I take this off, you'll give them back to me?"

"I don't want your necklace for myself. I just want you to take it off so you can stay," Mac said. "We're family, aren't we?"

I frowned. My heart ached for her in that moment. I understood loneliness. I understood being so desperate for connection that you'd do almost anything. But I didn't understand hurting other people to get it.

The fire hadn't actually burned anything. The fire *wasn't* burning anything. The things on the table looked burned, but Mac's illusions weren't strong enough for real flames. I took some steps forward, watching Mac, until I slid between Mac and the table. I kept my movements small to avoid Mac finding out what I was doing. *Please please please . . .*

"Okay," I said. "Okay. I'll take this off, but you have to let my friends go first. As soon as I know they're safe, I'll do it. I'll stay with you."

My hands felt around behind me, as frantic as I could manage without her noticing, until I felt what I was feeling for. Thin paper, thick paper, kind of curled up. The map. I held my breath while trying to roll it up behind my back. Mac stepped closer, and I froze.

"What are you doing?" she asked. Thunder rumbled.

I had to think fast. I didn't know the language the teachers had been chanting in. But I did know how the words sounded. If I could bluff my way through K-pop songs with Vee, I could take a whack at this chant. I took a deep breath, asked MawMaw Septine for help, and began.

CHAPTER 45

None of what I said sounded right. But it must have been good enough. Mac growled, sounding like thunder. She screamed, ranting in words I couldn't understand. She twitched and jerked and flailed. Her jerky backward gait into the shadows she had emerged from looked like a movie scene being played in reverse. I was terrified, but I kept repeating what I hoped were the right sounds until she was gone.

The flames around us faded into nothing. Something like peace blanketed the witching room.

I had done it. I had, somehow, put Mac to rest.

I tucked the map into the back of my pants and stepped toward the corner, now way less impossibly dark. The wood floor smoldered. A formless shape was burned into the planks. Like Mac had just . . . melted. She scared me, a lot, but still part of me felt empathy for her. Of course she was angry—she didn't deserve to die the way she had. I stooped down and placed a hand to the still-warm wood.

"I hope you're at peace," I said quietly.

I pushed my hands against the wall after standing up. I bounced in place to check the flooring. Nothing moved. So no way my friends fell through any weak spots somehow. The ceiling gave no clues, either. I sighed and picked up Lily's slippers. Hopefully they would be back at the dorm somehow. At least I could get Vee to help me search.

Oh crap, Vee. Was she still out there alone?

My steps felt heavy as I emerged from the witching room. I tried convincing myself that Ami, Theo, and Lily would be in my room when I got there. Or Theo's room. Or *anywhere* within Clearwater. Letting my brain do its spiraling thing would've been disastrous.

The library was deserted, which I expected.

I tested the revolving door to see if it was locked. Surprisingly, I spun around without resistance. I saw no sign of Vee after stepping outside. But the courtyard was speckled with people in bright orange T-shirts walking among dorm residents. No one acted as if anything strange had happened.

I crept closer. Without being too conspicuous, I trailed behind a girl who had goth vibes in every other aspect of her look besides the shirt. I stood close-ish so that I could read the front of the shirt.

BLYTHE ACADEMY CENTENNIAL CELEBRATION VOLUNTEER—ASK ME ANYTHING!

I weaved through volunteers setting up booths and assembling rides to head back to my dorm. The forest shuddered as I approached. Silence overshadowed the morning birdsong that had been trilling seconds earlier.

The trees dared me to come forward, to keep going on the path to Clearwater. It felt like an ambush. I heard, just barely, the cries of the dead as the forest darkened. Nowhere else—just the trees. I stepped back. The darkness crept closer. And closer. It spilled from the farthest trees and cascaded ever closer to me.

Clearwater became a blur in the distance as I ran the other way, praying to whoever or whatever might be listening to give me enough speed to outrun the shadows.

CHAPTER 46

Whenever life overwhelmed me and I didn't feel like I could talk to Daddy or Mama, I'd always turned to Auntie Nooncie. It didn't matter what I came to her with—she always knew exactly the right things to say. But being around the teacher version of her felt awkward. I didn't know how to balance Miss Noon and Auntie Nooncie. So I'd almost entirely kept her at a distance while here.

Right now, though, I needed Auntie Nooncie in the worst way. I just had to hope that after everything that had happened I could trust her.

I tried to avoid bumping people as I ran. Hurried apologies had to do. There wasn't time to stop and feel bad.

By the time I reached Miss Noon's cottage in the faculty housing, the sky was completely overcast. The little village of staff members who lived on campus wasn't too far from the library and courtyard but sat closer to the waterfall. I knocked on her door so hard I knew I'd bruise.

Miss Noon's forest-green door squealed open. We both startled as I nearly knocked her right on the head.

"Oh my goodness, Eva." She laughed quietly. She clutched her deep red bathrobe closed with one hand. I couldn't help but think about the tablecloth in the witching room. Same color. "What's—"

"Ami and Theo and Lily are gone! Mac took them!" Miss Noon blinked a few times, then glanced to the black sky. "Auntie Nooncie, *please*. Please help me."

"Eva . . . I don't—"

"No, I *know* you know what I'm talking about," I insisted. "I *saw* you! I saw *all* of you! You know this place is haunted and you're acting like I'm crazy! And now my friends are in some ghost dimension, probably being tortured, and I straight up vanished for an entire *night* apparently, and now I'm begging you to help me and you don't even care! You're supposed to believe me! You're supposed to be my safe person and you won't even tell me the truth! Did you know? Did you know Sutton would haunt me? Is that why you transferred?"

I waited for the inevitable—Miss Noon to laugh at me, tell Miss Alice I'd finally snapped, to call my dad, to kick me out of Blythe. But I stood tall and kept eye contact with her to let her know I meant business. It made my skin crawl, and I wanted to run again, but I stayed.

Eventually, she stepped aside.

The living room felt way too hot. I had to tell myself that Auntie Nooncie liked heat. It wasn't Mac. It couldn't be . . . I had seen her disappear; she was at rest now. After setting me up with a glass of water, Auntie Nooncie excused herself to her room with the promise that she'd return in less than five minutes.

Anita Baker sang like a siren over a quiet Bluetooth speaker near the spot on the loveseat I sank into. Auntie Nooncie and Mama had put me on to her as a kid, and I started to mumble along to keep myself present. With so much happening, I could feel myself starting to shut down, to drift into my own internal world. I needed to be in the moment. I needed to hold it together for my friends.

"Hey," Auntie Nooncie said. I could only barely hear her. So I slowly lowered the music down and turned. But she had her phone cradled in the crook of her neck, shoulder raised to hold it in place, and she wasn't talking to me. "Yeah, she just got here. Can you let the others know? Meet in the main courtyard in fifteen."

"Eva?" Vee stepped into the hallway, her voice sounding mouselike. Nothing like how she normally was.

As soon as I stood up, Vee broke into a run straight at me. She crashed against me, squeezed her arms around my neck a little too tightly. A swell of warmth came over me, a swirl of so many emotions crashing together. Relief, happiness, a little bit of fear still—I couldn't remember the last time I'd added new people to my safe list, but apparently I'd slid my new friends onto it without even realizing.

"Holy crow, I was so scared for you," she said. She sounded out of breath. Or ready to cry. Or both. "Nobody answered the walkie and I couldn't find anybody when I went in, and I didn't know what to do, and I didn't want to go back to our room alone, and you said Miss Noon is a friend of your family's so I thought . . ."

She shook hard enough that I rattled along with her. We'd never hugged before, but rather than push her away, I hugged her back. At least Vee was safe, if nobody else was.

CHAPTER 47

Fourteen minutes passed between getting to Auntie Nooncie's and returning to the library. That whole time, I worried. I worried we would be too late to help my friends. I worried that I hadn't said the right words to Mac. I worried that I *had* said the right words and that Mac was somewhere in the afterlife, lonely and in pain. I didn't bother wiping my tears away as we walked.

The other teachers we'd seen in the witching room were already waiting for us on the library steps by the time the three of us arrived. Miss Alice, permanently scowling, almost looked like a regular human adult with her hair in curlers and tied in a scarf. She stood with her arms folded, thick-framed glasses taking up nearly half her face. It surprised me to realize she must have normally worn contacts, since she seemed scary enough that she could spook her eyes into acting right with just a quirk of her eyebrow.

Just behind her, Miss Gloriana was ranting at someone in Spanish on a video call, hands gesturing to drive her points home. The contrast between her intense words and her extremely kawaii pajamas, covered in smiling clouds and angel cats, would've made me laugh if I didn't feel so upset about my missing friends.

"Oh, honey." Miss Eugenie frowned and gathered Vee and me into a hug. Though she very quickly let me go. "I'm so sorry. Habit. Can I . . . ?" I shook my head no, I didn't want a hug. "Okay. Okay, I respect that. So what's the plan, Noon?"

"I don't know," Auntie Nooncie admitted. "This is something I've never dealt with before. Protecting Eva is my priority. The familiarity the rest of you have with Sutton's spirit should've handled the rest."

"With respect, Miss Noon," Miss Alice snipped without any hint of respect, "Sutton has never once stolen any of my students in previous years."

"If you're trying to imply that this is Eva's fault—"

"Stop!" I yelled.

Anger flooded me. Everyone grew quiet and turned their attention to me. But I felt less anxious, less afraid, about the attention. I was too worried about my friends. Too full of rage over the terrible things the Friends put the sharecroppers through. How could they be arguing right now?

Miss Alice and Auntie Nooncie shared matching surprised looks. I shook, I was so overloaded with emotions.

"Our friends are *missing*," I reminded them. "It doesn't matter about fault. Blame me all you want. Just stop fighting and *do something!*"

A boom shook the courtyard and sounded like cannon fire. Volunteers screamed, Vee screamed, I clung to Auntie Nooncie. On the far side of the courtyard, another huge pop. Sparks arced out of an electric sign as each LED light exploded in sequence. A tall, gangly man hopped out of the way, yelling and flailing as part of his pants caught fire.

Auntie Nooncie rushed over to try and help calm the situation while Miss Alice barked orders to rein in the chaos. More electrical equipment exploded, shooting sparks and flames and mayhem. A food stall began to burn. I watched flames race up, across, throughout other structures in the courtyard. And then, the fire reached the stage.

This was it, I was right all along. Something disastrous *was* destined to hit the festival, and I was powerless to stop it. I had failed. I had unraveled some of the mystery behind Blythe's hauntings, but not enough. Not enough to save my friends, and not enough to prevent the tragedy that was unfolding before us now.

The stage, only half built, smoldered before a bigger flame burst toward the sky. My skin tingled as the heat swallowed all the air around me. A beam crackled and collapsed, and the goth-looking volunteer I'd followed earlier lost her footing on the stage as it shook and disappeared in the rubble before anyone could reach her.

Everything felt surreal. Like a thousand steps beyond dissociating. Like the wavy air was because of my own brain and not from just how screaming hot the fire was. I looked to Vee, and she was frozen, too.

Smoke puffed up toward the still-black sky. Thick and heavy and overwhelming. Vee began coughing and waving smoke away. Her mouth was moving, but I couldn't hear a word between the shouting, the roar of the fire, and my brain being way overstimulated. It took seconds for Vee to become completely swallowed by the smoke. It didn't make sense; there was way more smoke than there should have been. Not to mention, this smoke was behaving in ways that made even less sense. It shouldn't have weaved through the courtyard like it had an agenda.

My lungs burned with every breath. Yelling for Vee more just hurt me, so I quieted down. I tried to stumble toward where she'd been, but very quickly got lost, unable to find her. I couldn't see anyone at all—not Auntie Nooncie, not the volunteers or other students, not Miss Alice and her curlers. Soon, a darkness appeared within the gray clouds. Like a blister within the smoke. It looked so much like what I'd seen in the woods days earlier.

The dark core of the smoke spread more. It bubbled closer. Right before my eyes, that core morphed into more defined shapes, more humanlike. The roar of the fire changed into wails that I knew immediately would never leave me. Like the liquid in a lava lamp, the darkness began to separate. Wailing became screaming became distressed calls for help. I'd heard it before. And in that instant, I knew what was happening.

This wasn't smoke at all.

These were spirits.

Angry, confused, terrifically lonely spirits.

And the silhouette at the center of them all, the one I knew in my gut brought all this fire and destruction to Blythe—

"Mac."

CHAPTER 48

I whispered her name like a forbidden curse. Mac had done this. I'd been so naive to think I'd put her to rest just because she'd disappeared. She'd taken Theo, Lily, and Ami, and now Vee and Auntie Nooncie and everyone as far as I could see. She'd started this fire. And now she waited for the whole structure to collapse.

Her burned, rotting flesh didn't scare me this time. Neither did the cold, vacant staring. Whatever parts of her she'd left behind in me just felt fired up and ready to unleash hell. I stepped toward her but immediately froze. The ground began shaking beneath me. In an instant, the sky dumped what must've been four feet of rain right onto me all at once. The smoke around us melted away, but the fire kept spreading and the ghosts remained.

This was just another one of Mac's tricks, I realized. And tricks could always be revealed.

"Mac!" I screamed. She wasn't bothered by my tone at all. "Talk to me! Why are you doing this?"

Thunder crackled almost exactly as one lightning bolt after another zigged across the sky. Mac said nothing. She didn't show any hint that she'd even heard me at all. I started to doubt myself; maybe all this was *my* trick on myself. Something I'd dreamed up because of stress. But before I got further down that line of thinking, another violent shake of the ground jostled me hard enough that I landed knees-first on the concrete walkway.

It hurt so much I felt nauseous. My vision went white for a split second, and when it returned, Mac was gone. The smoke spirits had vanished. I tried standing, but that white-hot pain came back. That left me stuck doing an awkward half crawl, half drag across the courtyard toward the stage, where Mac had come from.

I didn't make it very far.

Another thunderous boom echoed, but this time it came from below me. In an instant, I felt weightless. Like I was falling. And it took me a few seconds to realize I actually *was* falling. I didn't have time to scream—the ground knocked the wind out of me.

I groaned, rolling onto one side. After a few deep breaths to prepare, I forced myself to stand. My hands groped air as I tried to get my bearings in near-total darkness.

Every few steps made me wince. I felt like a box full of broken glass; I just knew my insides must've been all messed up. I was in a cavernous hole in the ground in the middle of the court-yard, and water was rising quickly. I tried feeling for anything that could help me climb out. I couldn't get any grip on the dirt walls around me, especially as the downpour turned it all into disgusting, gloopy mud. So much stimulation made me dizzy, but I ignored the screaming in my brain begging me to just curl up and let the water take me. All the anger and frustration fueled me . . . at least for now. A meltdown would have to wait.

My third try in jumping up to pull myself out, I grabbed something solid within the mud. I put way too much faith in it—instead of holding me up, I yanked it out of the muddy wall and crashed down. The rock or root or whatever it was stabbed into my side. I screamed. And when I rolled to get off it, I screamed even more.

There, with a jagged bit of my shirt snagged onto its broken end, was a bone. I tried to scramble away, but the water was rising quickly, and it churned and sloshed the bone toward me. Another bone slid out of the mud wall and splashed beside me.

And another.

And another.

More and more bones shook loose from the sides of the pit, coming way too close to hitting me every time. I moved out of the way when I could, dodging slower and slower each time. Mud caked my clothes and my hair and beneath my nails. I wanted so badly to cry; I hated the feeling so much. My foot was stuck on something, and if the water kept rising I would drown. I reached down to try and yank my foot free, but more bones floated up. Screaming, I threw them aside and kept struggling in the mud. In my frantic efforts to escape, I elbowed something incredibly hard, like rock. Pins and needles tingled all the way up through my arm as I turned to see what I'd hit.

Sticking out of the mud, crooked and lumpy and hard, was a stone.

A gravestone.

Suddenly, I understood.

The bones, the hauntings, the gravestone—the Friends *hadn't* relocated the cemetery at all. At most, they'd simply moved a few headstones and called it a day.

Worse, I thought about the note we'd found in the witching room with the dots. It had to have been a list of all the places the Friends set on fire in order to get the sharecroppers to sell their land. They had felt so entitled to this land, even though people were already living here, that they terrorized the sharecroppers into leaving their homes, and then they hadn't even had the decency to move their cemetery before they began building on it.

I immediately felt a sense of anger for the sharecroppers and their families, even though they were tormenting me, trapping me in this hole. Daddy told Egypt and me many times about instances through American history that went down like this. White people wanting to take over land from Black and Indigenous people and doing whatever they could to get that land.

The ghosts had spent decades in unrest. No wonder they were so hostile.

I wanted to call out to them, to tell them I understood now, that I felt that soul-deep loneliness sometimes, too, and I could help them if they helped me. But the muddy water rose higher than my head. I couldn't swim against it; I felt like I was trapped in quicksand. Worse, something beneath the water tangled itself around me and made it impossible to get away. I didn't know if I even wanted to see what it was that held me.

Mud sliding down my throat and into my lungs made me feel like I was being suffocated with concrete. I couldn't catch my breath, I couldn't move, I couldn't see, I couldn't do anything except for wait for it to be over. I'd failed. I had been brave, but not brave enough. I would drown and join the sharecroppers in the afterlife, right here in this pit. That was what Mac wanted, anyway.

CHAPTER 49

No.

The thought was so strong, it overwhelmed me.

No. The word echoed in my head again, this time sounding like MawMaw Septine.

No. I heard the voices of Mama and Daddy and Egypt and even Dr. Choudhury.

No, Eva, don't give up. I didn't come all this way and learn to truly use my voice just to allow myself to drown. I had to keep fighting. No matter what.

With a surge of strength I didn't know I had, I kicked and yanked as hard as I could, finally freeing my foot from the mud. I fought through the muddy water until my head broke the surface. The rain pelted down on me as I gulped for air, my lungs screaming.

Above me—or maybe below, nothing made sense anymore— muffled chanting grew louder and louder. In an instant, I knew what it was. Auntie Nooncie, Miss Alice, Miss Eugenie, Miss Gloriana—they chanted together, the same words we'd caught them saying in the witching room. The same words I'd messed up that led me right into this hole.

They were trying to save me. And I'd almost given up on saving myself. Their care for me bolstered my fight instincts. With the water rising so high, I was almost close enough to the top of the pit to slog my way out if I put my back into it. The mud burned my eyes with every blink, but I could make out rough shapes.

I started to think I might just make it.

When we first saw them chanting, it had felt like they were doing something bad. But if Miss Noon was chanting now, I knew it must be some kind of spell to protect me. If they thought it would help . . . I joined the chanting as best as I could, imagining that the rhythm of the words would give me strength.

I managed to reach the edge of the pit, and my nails scraped against the concrete, hurting even worse than hitting my knees had. I felt sick, but I pulled myself as hard as I could, grunting and groaning and screaming my way up and out of the pit. I could feel hands gripping my face, pulling me in for a hug, and even with the mud in my eyes I could tell it was Vee.

The intense rain began to wash away the mud covering me. I tried to cough, but my heaving stomach forced out the mud I'd swallowed instead. I vomited violently on the ground. And the chanting continued all the while.

It took all my strength to push myself off the ground, and even with some support from Vee, I still felt like I might topple right back over. Auntie Nooncie watched me like she wanted to run over and help, too, but all she could do was stand hand in hand with the other teachers.

Smoke started to envelop the courtyard again. It covered the ruined stage, billowed up around Auntie Nooncie, the scared volunteers, me. Everything was smoky and wet and confusing. The thicker the smoke got, the louder the teachers chanted. And the louder they chanted, the louder the smoke wailed.

The smoke spirits started to take form once more. I anticipated it this time. I held on to Vee's hand and tried not to be so scared about whatever was coming toward us. This time, instead of seeing dozens of skeletal faces, I saw my own.

Or, Mac's, actually. Her burned, scarred face. But seeing her, I could see myself. I could see Nanay. I could see similarities that I hadn't noticed before. In that instant, I knew. I hadn't been seeing just Mac in my visions; Mac and Nanay were intertwined, just like Mac and me right now. Mac attached to us because we felt familiar to her. She was family. All she wanted was family. I knew that feeling, too, how it could burn so deep it felt fatal.

How lonely it felt without that support. How hard it was to feel unheard, unseen.

There was something in her expression—something like need, mixed with regret. Fear and pain. It clicked for me—all the anger, the sadness, the intensity I felt wasn't just mine. It was hers, too. She was hurting us, and whatever power was behind our chanting was hurting her, too.

We stared at each other, and it felt like we understood each other completely in that moment. Mac was just a scared kid, like me. One who had died terribly, and been lonely, and now was full of rage and power. I didn't want to hurt her anymore, even if it would help myself.

Vee gripped my hand tightly, but I was fixated on Mac. I breathed in, then let go of Vee and took a careful step toward Mac.

"Make them stop chanting," I said to Vee. "Trust me."

I took another careful step in Mac's direction and held out my hand to her. I waited for her to take it.

"Please please please please," I whispered to myself. "C'mon . . ."

Mac crept forward, and we nearly touched fingertips. Somehow, I wasn't scared of Mac anymore. I knew that if I could just be there for her, if I could comfort her, help dispel some of the pain she felt, all this could end. I stretched a little more to get to her. Mac lifted her arm and reached to me. Singed pieces of flesh flaked off, little sparks drifting to the ground. I smiled as best I could to try and put her at ease. This was it. This was the end. We'd make everything better and the hauntings would stop.

And I was sure of that, so sure, until every cell in my body exploded with a pain I had never felt before.

CHAPTER 50

I must've been struck by lightning. It was the only explanation for why I felt like my blood had been replaced with millions of sewing needles trying to push their way out of my skin. I could see Mac, not far from me, screeching and convulsing. Auntie Nooncie and the others moved closer. I could see Vee pleading with them to stop, but instead their chants changed to something else, something I hadn't heard before. But every word of it made the needles in me multiply.

Mac seemed to be doing just as bad as me. No matter how scared she'd made me, I didn't want her to be in this much pain, too.

"Stop!" I yelled. It was more of a croak, but I tried to be as loud as I could manage. "Stop! You're hurting her!"

More screaming, more lightning. A magnolia toppled over. It slammed across the stage, right on top of some electrical equipment.

"Auntie Nooncie, please," I gasped. She stuttered in her chanting and looked at Miss Alice for a second. "Help me! *Please*, stop! You're killing us!"

"Stop!" Vee yelled in support. Panic painted her drenched face as she started to tug on Auntie Nooncie's arm.

It took more yelling from both Vee and me, and it felt like seven lifetimes, but the chants stopped. The pain faded. And Mac and I stared at each other as we lay on the ground. She was weak; the storm let up second by second and I could almost see right through her. Seeing her like that made me feel horrible. I had to try and make it better.

"If I stay, will you promise not to scare anyone?" I asked. "Or hurt anyone? And you'll give my friends back?"

Mac just stared. I thought she might refuse, but instead, she looked at me with solemn eyes. "Tell the truth."

Finally, the pieces came together. "I will," I promised her. "I'll make sure everyone knows the truth of what happened to your family. *Our* family. They won't be able to lie about it ever again. And I'll make sure your cemetery is treated with respect from now on."

A look of peace washed over Mac's face, like a thousand-pound weight had lifted off her shoulders. She gave a small nod, just as she started to fade away completely. The smoke around us dissipated. Overhead, the sky lightened back to a more normal shade. All that was left behind of the whole thing was a busted-up festival stage.

I could still hear shouting and distant sirens, and I saw Vee staring down at me. I winced as I tried to sit up. I stared at the grove of magnolias as if they could make sense of this for me. And I could have sworn I saw Mrs. Perrin slowly disappearing into the woods. This time, seeing her made me feel . . . peaceful.

"Oh my God, there are so many bones!" Miss Eugenie's yelling interrupted my serenity. Miss Gloriana, meanwhile, was speaking loudly and swearing now and then. I tried laughing at how ridiculous they probably looked, but moving even a little bit hurt my ribs.

So when I heard three quick whistles and jumped to my feet to follow the sound, I knew I'd majorly regret it later. But it didn't matter. I knew that sound. It *had* to be Ami. Vee must have had the same thought, since she ran with me.

Ami climbed out of the pit with our help. Mud coated them all over but they smiled hugely, anyway, and reached back to help Lily scramble out, too. Theo, last to be rescued, immediately began crying when she surfaced.

I was so happy to see them it felt like my heart would burst. As soon as all three of them were out of the pit, I hugged them tighter than I'd ever hugged anybody not blood related to me. Even the hug hurt, and not because of my touch issues this time.

I was grateful, but I was also exhausted and sad and angry. The rain had stopped, but I felt hot tears on my cheeks. I was just so excited to have my friends back; I could forget about the pain. Kinda. A little.

Almost as soon as we stopped hugging, the pain hit me again. I started to scream. In pain, sure, but also because everything that had happened left so many feelings in me that it felt like yelling was the only way to get them out. I screamed for Ami, and Theo, and Lily. I screamed for those miserable, lonely, forgotten spirits buried beneath our school. I screamed for the disrespect they had been shown and their erasure. I screamed just to scream. To use my voice and not be afraid of it.

Vee tried to calm me. But it didn't matter. I needed to yell. Better, I *wanted* to. And I knew nothing would ever stop me from doing it again.

CHAPTER 51

The hospital gave me strong pain meds and a strawberry fruit juice Popsicle, so it almost made me feel back to normal. And it felt pretty good to sit in my hospital bed and marathon home renovation shows after getting my knee shoved back into place. By the time I got released, I was pretty sure I'd wind up living in a split-story Craftsman house with subway tiling and ship-lap everywhere someday. The whole ride back to campus with Auntie Nooncie, I daydreamed about paint swatches.

"Eva!"

As soon as I crutched into my dorm room, Ami and Vee both wrapped me up in a massive hug. I almost lost my balance; I'd never used crutches before and I still felt kind of wobbly from the really strong medication I'd been given. But I managed to hold myself up and use one arm to hug them, too.

Across the way, Theo sat on Vee's bed. She smiled at me and waved a little. Bruises marked up her skin, and scratches and scrapes were on her face. And yet, she was still beautiful. Lily, from the floor in front of the bed, elbowed Theo's leg like they were sharing a secret.

"All right, Doods," Auntie Nooncie said. She started petting my hair. "If you need me, just give me a call, okay? Tomorrow, we can call your parents and fill them in. Make sure you girls get some sleep. You were all very brave today."

With a quick kiss to my forehead, Auntie Nooncie backed out of the room and shut the door behind her. I made my way toward my bed, but Ami redirected me to sit next to Theo. I was a little disoriented and too tired to resist. I didn't expect her to move closer to me, and I especially didn't expect her to hug me, too. I froze. I didn't even breathe. After a few seconds, she let me go.

"Thanks," Theo said once she let me go. "For working so hard to save us."

"Three cheers for Eva, the bravest little bean in town!" Ami climbed onto Vee's bed and plopped down to sit behind Theo. They took hold of one of my hands. "A literal ghostbuster."

"A ghostbuster detective," Vee added. She sat down near Lily.

"We could open an agency," I added quietly. The others all laughed, and it felt pretty good to hear. "Why are you guys all in here?"

"Well, there was no way any of us were staying alone," Ami said. "And we all wanted to make sure you got back okay."

I felt even better hearing that. I smiled some. "I'm really tired," I said.

"Oh yeah, of course," Vee said.

The others scrambled to get out of the way. Ami and Lily helped tuck me into my bed and then Ami decided to share with Vee. Theo and Lily created a makeshift bed on the floor in between us. Sleeping on my back was going to be the worst, but at least I'd already gotten some lounge clothes before getting out of the hospital. I wouldn't have to get changed.

Vee cut the lights and I almost immediately felt myself fluttering off to sleep. I tried to will myself to stay awake for even a few more minutes to talk with my friends.

My friends. That felt good, too. I knew now that if I could survive the events of the last couple of weeks, I could survive anything Blythe could throw at me. My family had freaked out about my accident and Daddy had offered to come get me, but I'd told him I was okay on my own. I had the strength of MawMaw Septine's memory bolstering me. And I had my friends. I would be okay.

"Tomorrow's the centennial," Lily said, almost in a whisper. The hum of the air conditioner was the only response at first.

"I think I'm good on Halloween for now," I said.

"Yeah . . . How about we just . . . don't?" Vee suggested.

An awkward vein of laughter spread through us. I wanted to say more, to ask about where they'd vanished to, or to ask what they thought we could do to make sure the cemetery would be properly respected going forward. But I kept quiet, and several minutes passed before deep, rhythmic breathing filled the room. Somehow, I wasn't the first to fall asleep.

It didn't take long before I was awake alone. My heart sped up. I almost expected something to happen now that no one else was awake to see. But things were done, I reminded myself. Mac promised to behave. Nothing was going to happen. And I'd keep my side of the promise, too.

I had to talk to Miss Alice and the others as soon as I felt up to it. I knew I had to make sure Mac and the sharecroppers were laid to rest properly. They needed a new cemetery, maybe some plaques around town. And the school needed to tell the truth about its history. The teachers had thought they'd been doing the right thing by using a spell to try to bind Mac's powers, that doing so could keep the students safe. But all they'd done was make Mac more and more desperate to be heard.

And I even felt grateful to be related, even distantly, to Mac. If she hadn't felt our family connection and zeroed in on me, I never would have been able to help her. Everything that happened was worth it because it brought the truth to light. I started to wonder if the Friends had any remaining family members around that I could speak to.

And I *would* speak to them.

Thoughts of how to make things up to Mac, to Mrs. Perrin, to the people whose land was stolen, swirled in my sleepy brain. Considering how difficult it would be for Miss Alice to explain all this, I had the upper hand in getting a memorial done for them.

"I'm sorry about what happened to you," I said aloud to no one in particular. "I'm going to make triple sure the city builds you a new cemetery. So you can rest peacefully. But no more scaring people, okay?"

Part of me expected someone to answer. When no one did, I let out a relieved sigh. I hoped that meant the hauntings were over.

I started to turn over to lie on my side, but my giant cast reminded me I was pretty well stuck. All I could do was turn my head, at least. Which left me staring straight at my closet. I felt nervous about seeing the closet and what might come out of it. But I channeled Brave Ghostbuster Detective Eva and stayed right where I was.

"Good night, ghosts," I muttered.

Just before I nodded off, I swore, for a second, the closet door squeaked open.

THE END.

Acknowledgments

Eva came to me easily. Almost fully formed, even. I could picture her as clear as day in my head before I'd even written a single word. The rest, unfortunately, was more of a struggle. Not because the story itself was hard—this was actually the easiest time I'd had writing a novel in years. But because the rest of life decided to be as brutally overwhelming, angering, and depressing as possible. So many world-changing things happened in the time between conceptualizing the story and you reading this right now. Not even my name is the same as it had been at the start of this journey.

So often, I thought about giving up. I thought I would simply say, "Never mind," and delete this whole book, and every other project I was working on, and walk into the forest to live as a hermit with only woodland creatures to keep me company. But that would have been easy(ish). That would have been the opposite of what Eva would do. No matter how scared or frustrated Eva might get, she's never one to give in to those feelings. No matter what. And I thought to myself that I needed that same level of resolve to get through the worst of what life wanted to throw at me.

And somehow—I did it. I got through the bad times, the mad times, the sad times, and I stayed true to myself. And for that, I'm proud of me. I don't often take the time to acknowledge that kind of thing for myself, even though I'll readily sing the praises of loved ones for any minor achievement they might experience. So this time, I'm choosing to acknowledge myself first. I'm proud that I survive moments when I think I might sink. I'm proud that I know when and how to ask for a life vest from other trusted humans. I'm proud that I'm able now to say that I'm proud of me without feeling awkward or boastful.

I invite you, reader, to take pride in yourself as well. You've lived through every one of your worst days. You're still here. You have reason to celebrate that fact, even if maybe it doesn't feel like it right now. You're doing your best, despite what it may feel like. And whatever you might be going through—be it school, work, friends, family, romance, health—you'll get through that, too. Eva and I believe in you.

Special thanks to everyone who made this book possible— the whole team at Scholastic who believed in this book, and in particular my lovely, patient, brilliant editor, Maya Marlette. My agent, Jim McCarthy. My friends who were forced to listen and brainstorm and share opinions. My cats. My fish and frogs and snails and shrimp. My mom.

This book includes some topics that I strongly suggest

readers explore outside of their time reading Eva's story. Look into the history of sharecroppers and the Reconstruction era. Look into local history. Talk to loved ones who may have first- or secondhand knowledge—it might seem like a very long time ago, but it's barely a blink of an eye in terms of the history of the universe. Take the time to honor the people who endured such hardships, discuss their struggles, and keep their memories close to heart.

About the Author

g. haron davis is a New York–born, Tennessee-raised author, cat parent, and fishkeeper. Currently residing in the outskirts of Kansas City, Missouri, they specialize in horror and fantasy with a little bit of funny thrown in for good measure. In their spare time, they can be found playing video games, daydreaming about epic fish tank builds, and preaching the gospel of BTS. They can be found online at ghdis.me and @mxgeeTV on Twitter, Instagram, Threads, and TikTok.